SEX ON THE MAT

Edited By

ERIC SUMMERS

Herndon, VA

Published in the United States by STARbooks Press

PO Box 711612, Herndon, VA 20171

Many thanks to graphic artist John Nail for the cover design.

Mr. Nail may be reached at: tojonail@bellsouth.net.

Contents

OUT ON THE MAT
By Logan Zachary

Logan Zachary (LoganZachary2002@yahoo.com or www.loganzacharydicklit.com) lives in Minneapolis, MN. His new books available and he has more than 100 stories in various anthologies.

Sweat burned Adam's eyes as the hand grabbed his balls and pushed his face into the floor. He spread his legs and extended his whole body trying to break the hold that held him. The pelvis pushed against his ass, and Adam felt the bulge enter between his cheeks. His tender hole puckered under its assault, and he felt his cock start to swell. This wasn't the right time for a boner.

"If you want a gold medal, you're gonna have to fight for it," his coach said.

The hand pressed on his hairy sac. Adam felt his arousal grow. How could he fight and escape if he was so horny and turned on? He had to focus, he had to ...

The coach lifted his body up and flung him over onto the mat.

Adam rolled onto all fours and sprang up. He pounced and grabbed at the hairy legs that stood over him.

His opponent thrust his legs back and his pelvis down to widen his stance.

Adam's arms couldn't hold his legs, and they slipped through his hands. He felt his coach roll over his body and wrap his arms around Adam's waist. One hand brushed along his hard shaft and held onto his fat mushroom head. Adam wanted to die of embarrassment as he struggled to escape. He dropped to the mat and spread his arms and legs wide to break the bond that held him. Sweat poured off his body, which helped him start to slip away. His red spandex singlet rode up his butt crack and gave him a wedgie.

Coach's arms slipped down his narrow waist, and Adam wiggled free. He spun in mid-air and landed on his coach's back. He could feel the strong muscles underneath him, despite his being more than twice his age. Coach had gone to the Olympics and had a gold metal to show for it.

Adam hoped one day he would, too.

"Adam, I think that's enough for today." Coach said and wiped his hands on his legs. "I think I know what your problem is, and I think I have a way of fixing it."

Adam swallowed hard. He had a problem? Crap. What was wrong with him?

Coach took out a small notebook and wrote a quick note on a sheet. "Here is my address, come over to my house tomorrow morning around ten in the morning. We'll work on your problem then." He handed him the paper and headed off to his office.

Adam rose and grabbed his towel and headed to the locker room. It was late Friday night, and most of the other college students had left for the day.

He dropped his stuff off at his locker and slipped out of his singlet. He rolled it up and tossed the sweat damp thing into his bag. He pulled his jock off and threw that in there, too. He hoped he had a clean one at his dorm; otherwise he'd be washing clothes tonight.

He tossed his towel over his shoulder and headed to the shower room. His erection was semi-hard and flopped in front of him. He heard the water running and quickly pulled his towel down in front of his body to hide his arousal.

As he rounded the doorway, he saw coach's hairy body standing under a shower head. His hairy back, butt, and legs made him look like a bear. His curly gray hair darkened in the spray, making him look younger. His body was still sculpted and firm, just a little rounder in the center.

Adam watched as Coach soaped his body up and let the water cascade over him and down the drain. He soaped his front and slowly turned to face the spray.

Adam almost gasped when he saw the Coach's huge uncut cock. It hung from between his legs like a third leg. His chest and torso were hairy, too.

Coach stroked along his thick shaft, washing his dick. He pulled back on the foreskin and a pink tip slipped out. He soaped his cock and then worked down to his low hanging balls. He looked like a bull in the shower. Coach opened his eyes and smiled as he saw Adam standing there. "The water feels great at the end of the day." He turned his back to Adam and soaped between his hairy butt cheeks.

Adam hung his towel on a hook and raced for a shower. He spun the dial and stepped under the spray before it was warm. He wanted the cold shock to help shrink his erection. He watched carefully as the Coach finished his shower and turned off the water. He turned his back to coach as he walked to retrieve his towel.

Coach dried his hair and came to stand by Adam as he soaped up. "Do you have plans for tonight?"

Adam almost jumped out of his skin. He hadn't heard the Coach come to talk to him. He spurted out water from his mouth and said, "No plans." He kept his back to him as he spoke, pretending to rinse off his front.

"Well, have a great night." Coach wiped down his chest and walked back to his office in the locker room.

Adam exhaled the air he had been holding. He had never seen the coach shower here before. He soaped up his chest and washed lower. He could feel his excitement return, but he quickly soaped, rinsed and got out of the shower. Adam wrapped the towel around his waist and headed back to his locker. His wet feet slapped on the concrete floor. When he opened his locker, he couldn't find his underwear. Crap. He bent over, and his towel fell off.

He dropped to his knees and felt under the locker for his briefs.

"You have a bruise on your right cheek," Coach said.

Adam's face burned as he fumbled to pull his towel around himself. "I must have landed wrong."

"Well, have a great night and see you tomorrow morning." Coach picked up his gym bag and headed out the door.

Adam sat down on the wooden bench and closed his eyes. What had the Coach seen wrong with him? Could he fix it? Or was he always going to be an average wrestler? And why did the Coach want him to come to his house? Did he know he was gay? How could he not with a raging hard-on in his pants when the Coach touched him.

Did the Coach want to …?

Adam lay back on the bench and brought his hand down to his lap. He liked hairy guys, but Coach was old enough to be his father. The Coach was married, wasn't he? But why would he want him at his house? Why not here at the gym? Maybe he was going to fire him from his instruction. Shit. If he lost his scholarship, he'd be booted out of college, and then what?

His hand worked between the folds of the damp towel, and he felt his hairy balls. His cock slowly grew. He ran a finger along his growing shaft and the dampness made his finger slide easily. He traced along the underside and over the fat mushroom head. A little fluid seeped out of the opening at the tip. He circled the end, spreading the pre-cum around and around.

His fingers grasped his cock and slowly stroked up and down, as he thought about the Coach's huge cock. He licked his lips before biting on his lower lip. His hand slipped up and down faster, knocking one side of his towel off his lap and exposing one leg. He felt his balls slip between his hairy legs and land on the damp towel. His hand worked faster, and the other side of the towel fell away. He spread his legs wider and slipped his other hand between his legs. He dug underneath his balls and fingered along his taint. His fingertip slid along the crease and found the tight pucker. The

5

moisture from the shower made his finger glide easily around his hole. He pushed into the opening as his other hand jacked faster and harder.

His legs rose up, and he felt the strain increase his pleasure across his body. More pre-cum oozed out of his cock and added lubrication to stroke faster.

His finger entered him as he thumbed his balls. He felt them start to pull up as the excitement grew. His breathing increased as he squeezed harder with his other hand. More pre-cum flowed out of him and along his shaft.

He fingered his butt deeper and harder as his other hand jacked faster and faster. His balls rose and an eruption rolled out of the hairy sac and sprayed across his belly. Wave after wave of come flowed out of his balls and sprayed across his torso; he jacked harder, milking each drop out of him. His finger entered deeper and tapped his prostate, triggering another wave to shoot out of him. His legs spasmed and slowly lowered to the floor as the warm, calm pleasure flowed over his whole body.

He lay there for a while as his body returned back to normal. He felt his load liquefy and flow off his body. He picked up his towel ends and cleaned himself up. He slowly sat up and slipped on his sweat pants. He stepped into his shoes and grabbed his T-shirt. He stuffed everything into his bag and headed back to his dorm.

# # # # #

Adam's roommate, Larry Lockwood, was a hockey player from Canada. He usually sat around their room in just his jock or underwear. He was a hairy, beefy guy, but skated like lightning on the ice. He was also being shortlisted for the Olympic hockey team. As he opened the door, Adam half expected to be greeted by his hairy ass framed in his wooden chair at the desk, but no one was in the room. Larry was a handsome guy, so Adam didn't mind the lack of clothing; besides, their room was always hot.

He tossed his gym bag on the bed and unzipped it. Adam dug out the sweaty damp clothes and tossed them into the laundry basket in the closet. He opened his top dresser drawer and pulled out a fresh jock, a new singlet, and a clean towel. He jammed them into the bag and zipped it closed. It was all set for tomorrow.

Why did Coach want him to come to his house? He'd find out tomorrow. With this meeting looming over his head, Adam felt he couldn't go out to the bars or the frat house for a few beers. He couldn't concentrate enough to think about his classes, so what to do?

He lay on his bed and closed his eyes.

# # # # #

The next thing Adam knew, the overhead light blazed on, and the door room burst open. Larry came in. He had been drinking and brought home company. So much for sleep tonight.

"Sorry, man. Didn't realize you were sleeping."

A girl giggled, and a guy swore.

Larry flipped the desk light on and turned off the room light.

Adam brought his arm down and rolled onto his side. Glancing at the alarm clock, he saw it was nine, but he wondered why it was so bright outside. "Are you guys going out?"

The girl jumped onto Larry's bed. "We're just getting in."

"What?" Adam jumped up and realized he had slept all night. He grabbed his toothbrush and towel. No one was in the restroom. He jumped into the shower with his toothbrush in his mouth. He washed quickly and dried off. To save time, he wore the same sweats from yesterday. He didn't want to change in the room with an audience. He threw his towel over the desk chair and grabbed his gym bag.

"Where are you off to?" Larry asked from his bed. The girl, the guy, and he were all naked under the sheets.

Adam paused for a second and held back the smirk that tried to escape. "Coach needed me for a special training."

"That doesn't sound good." Larry licked down the girl's neck, as the guy disappeared under the sheets. "Don't be late."

He grabbed his gym bag and ran out of the room. Adam found his car and tossed the bag in the passenger's seat and took off across town. Coach lived in the burbs, and he knew the neighborhood. He pulled up in front of the house at ten to ten.

Coach opened the door before he turned off his car. Not a good sign.

Adam raced up the stairs and across his porch. "Sorry, I'm late."

"Did you have breakfast?" Coach asked as he entered his home.

"I'm not a breakfast kind of guy."

Coach shook his head and nodded to the couch. "Have a seat." He disappeared into the kitchen. His living room was dark wood and overstuffed furniture. A huge fireplace covered one wall, and a picture window looked out to the street. He returned with a yogurt, a banana, and a glass of orange juice. "You can't work on an empty stomach."

Embarrassed, Adam accepted his food and ate quickly. He wanted to ask Coach what his problem was, but he waited. He knew the Coach wouldn't speak until he saw he was almost done with his breakfast.

"When you're done, we'll head downstairs to the basement. I have a gym down there." Coach pointed down the dark hallway.

Adam slow rose to his feet and picked up his gym bag. At least, he had told Larry where he was going, in case he disappeared. That is, if Larry remembered with all the alcohol and distractions in his bed. He had seen too many horror movies not to think of *Silence of the Lambs*.

Coach led him downstairs and turned on the lights as he went. The air became humid and close.

Adam inhaled deeply as he descended. No dead decaying bodies. Then the thought struck him, what if the Coach had a dungeon down here. Slings, handcuffs, and such.

As the last light came on, Adam turned the twist in the stairs and saw the floor of the basement was covered in gym mats. A wall was covered in wood and a wooden door read "SAUNA".

Coach stepped to the side and let Adam pass.

Adam kicked off his shoes before he stepped onto the mat. He dropped his bag and looked to the sauna door. "Should I change in there?"

Coach held up his hand and reached into his pocket. He pulled out a cell phone. He flipped it open and pressed a few buttons.

Adam wondered if he wanted to take pictures, but he saw the phone was ringing.

The phone beeped. "Yeah, he's here. Okay." Coach clicked the phone closed and turned to Adam. "Sorry to be so mysterious, but I wanted you to come here."

Adam swallowed hard.

"I'm sure there are a million of thoughts running through your mind, from does he want to eat me to does he want to fuck me."

Adam almost gasped.

"I know you have a great athletic talent, and I want you to succeed."

"But."

"But you have a problem we need to address."

Footsteps sounded on the stairs coming down to join them.

Adam and Coach looked up and watched someone down the steps. Bare feet, hairy bare legs, the swing of a robe, and a knee exposed from the slit in the robe. Another two steps and a handsome young guy came into view. He looked like Coach only younger.

"Adam, this is my son, Gabe."

Gabe stepped onto the mat and extended his hand.

Adam took it and shook it.

"Gabe is an excellent wrestler, too, and he can help you with your problem."

"And what is that?" Adam asked.

Coach turned and started up the stairs. "You guys will figure it out." He touched Gabe's shoulder. "Help him and help yourself." He continued up the stairs, at the top, he closed the door.

Adam turned to Gabe, "Do you know what my problem is?"

Gabe gave him a strange smile and said, "My dad wants me to wrestle with you and help you find out."

Adam shrugged and bent over to get his bag. "Did you want me to suit up?"

"No. I want you to get ready, but not suit up."

Adam laughed. "What do you mean?"

Gabe untied his robe and slowly let it open.

Adam's eyes widened as he saw that he was naked underneath.

The robe slipped off his shoulders and pooled around his feet. His body was exactly like Coach's, hairy, muscular, and extremely hung. His uncut cock, swung back and forth as did his low hanging hairy balls. "He wants us to wrestle in the nude, just like they did at the first Olympics."

"Naked?" Adam took a step back.

"Naked." Gabe stepped forward and turned around to pick up his robe. He folded it in half and placed it over the railing. He stepped in front of Adam and waited.

"I can't."

"Just take off your clothes and try."

Adam could feel his arousal grow and swell. His sweatpants tented easily since he still hadn't put on a pair of underwear.

"This is part of your training. Just try it. We can stop at anytime."

"I have a problem." And as soon as he said it, he knew why he was here. Coach had figured it out and now he knew. How could he compete? His options for the Olympics were over.

Gabe reached forward and touched both of his shoulders. "It's fine. I volunteered to do this, and I don't mind." His cock started to grow. "I'm gay also, and I can help." He reached under the bottom of the sweatshirt and pulled it up in front, as it came to eye level, he stopped and waited.

Adam shut his eyes and raised his arms.

Gabe pulled the sweatshirt off and folded it over the railing with his robe. He stepped back and pointed at his sweats. "Let's get started." He turned his back to Adam. "If you don't take them off, I will."

Adam laughed.

"Why did you laugh?" Gabe asked.

"You sound so much like your dad." And he checked out his ass, and knew he looked like him, too.

"Thank you, are they off?"

Adam held his waistband, still unsure. He pulled it out and looked at his erection.

"I know you're hard. I've seen the bulging sweats." He slowly turned.

Adam stood still, unsure of what to do.

13

Gabe pounced. He lowered his body and grabbed for the sweats as he wrapped his arms around his legs.

Adam tried to escape but couldn't. He threw his legs back in an attempt to get away but only ended up turning in Gabe's arms and going down to the mat. He twisted hard and felt his sweatpants slide off his ass.

Gabe grabbed the elastic waistband and pulled down harder. His hand played across his hairy butt on the way down.

Adam felt the waistband drop lower in the front and his cock sprang free from their confinements.

Gabe swiveled perpendicular to his body and worked the sweats the rest of the way down his legs.

Adam kicked and fought, but his pants only trapped his legs more.

Gabe laid his naked body over Adam's ass and pulled one leg free. He didn't let go of the sweats, and it only took one more tug, and they were off.

Adam tried to cover his naked body and hug the mat, but Gabe had other ideas. He leveled his arm underneath his body and started to flip him on his back.

Adam's cock swelled to full hard-on, and he fought even harder not to expose it. He tightened his whole body and tried to log roll the other way.

Gabe's arm reached between his hairy legs and flipped him with one swift motion.

14

The air in his lungs burst out, and his cock slapped against his belly with the force of landing on his back. His tip left a wet spot just under his belly button.

Gabe smiled down at him. "Very nice. I can see why you are struggling so much." His hand caressed along Adam's thick shaft and stroked it several times.

Waves of pleasure flowed over Adam's body, and his balls threatened to explode right then and there.

Gabe's hand cupped his balls and pulled on them. He rolled the fleshy orbs between his fingers. He released them, and let his hand glide from his balls, along his taint to the tender hole between his cheeks.

Adam bucked his hips and broke free from Gabe. He rolled away and started to get to his feet.

Gabe did a flying tackle and landed on his back. His cock slip along Adam's crease as his arms pinned Adam's hands to the floor. He gave Adam's butt a few pelvic thrusts.

Adam wanted it so bad, but he had to get away from him. His mind whirled in so many directions.

"You have a hot ass." Gabe whispered into his ear. "I want it."

Adam freaked, but Gabe's hold held him in place.

"Adam, relax." Gabe held him firmly; he knew that he had to just hold him until he calmed down. "I don't want to hurt you, but I can't let you go until you relax, I don't want to hurt you." He squeezed him hard once and relaxed to let him know he was serious.

Adam strained with all his might, but he couldn't escape. His panic sapped his strength. He continued to struggle but knew it was useless. He finally let go and flopped on the mat.

Gabe pulled him to his body and hugged him.

Adam burst into tears and sobbed heavily.

"That's alright, let it all out. You're fine. Let it out." Gabe caressed him and held him close.

Adam curled up into his arms and accepted his care. He hugged Gabe back, holding him for all he's worth.

"It's fine to be a gay athlete. You just have to come to terms with your sexuality and remove it when you wrestle. Remember to use your sex when you have some intimate time." Gabe's hand massaged down his legs and caressed over his butt. His circles grew bigger and bigger.

Adam twisted his pelvis to open himself up more as Gabe's hand worked over his body, exploring. He turned his head to face him — finally.

Gabe brought his full mouth down on Adam's and kissed him, gently at first and slowly his lips parted and suck his tongue out and slowly entered his mouth. Their tongues touched and fire ignited. Their hands explored and grabbed, groped and rubbed.

They rolled into each other's arms, and their pelvises pressed against each other. Their erections slid back and forth, alongside each other. Their passion grew as did the intensity.

Gabe broke their kiss and licked down his neck; he moved down to a nipple and took it into his mouth. He rolled the point between his teeth and sucked on it. The hair tickled his lips.

He tasted Adam and savored it.

Adam let go of him as Gabe kissed and licked lower. His chin ran along Adam's treasure trail and brushed the tip of his cock. He licked down the crease between his body and his testicle. He pulled the hairy ball into his mouth and tried to swallow it.

Adam threw his head back and spread his legs wide.

Gabe's nose inhaled the male musk of his balls and moved over to the other one. He teased it with his tongue.

Adam's dick throbbed above him, and he touched his tongue to the base of it, slowly, inch by inch, he licked along the thick shaft.

Adam's toes curled as his hands fisted.

Gabe hesitated at the fat wet tip. He breathed on it, making it dance under his breeze.

"Do it," Adam whispered, "do it."

Gabe kissed the moist tip and opened his mouth; he sucked the pre-cum out of the hole and then swallowed him whole. He gagged at the end but swallowed again. He sucked down on it and felt Adam's body open up. He slipped a finger between his ass cheeks and explored that tight pucker. The sweat made it slip easily inside. As he fingered his butt, he sucked on his cock.

Adam couldn't take the pleasure for much longer. He grabbed Gabe's hair and guided his head. Holding it back and having him linger over the sweet spot. More pre-cum flowed out of his cock.

Gabe swallowed as much as he could, but some escaped down his chin. He wiped it away with the back of his other hand. He thrust in deeper and tickled his prostate, milking out more sweet fluid.

"Fuck me," Adam begged.

Gabe slowly allowed his dick to escape his full lips and pulled out of his bottom. He stood and raced to the cabinet next to the sauna to return with a condom and a bottle of lube. He slipped the condom on and greased his hand and cock, before lifting up Adam's ass.

Adam grabbed his ankles and spread his legs wide. His pink pucker quivered with excitement. He wanted this; he needed this so badly.

Gabe rose up on his knees and guided his thick uncut dick into place. He rubbed the end over the opening to relax it to accept his girth. The tip pressed forward as his hand grabbed Adam's cock. He stroked along the shaft as he pushed forward.

The pressure grew, and Adam doubted this would work, but the hand on his dick, relaxed him. Slowly, his butt opened and accepted the thick intruder. The fat head stretched him for a few seconds of pain, only to engulf it when the head popped through.

Gabe rocked his hips back and forth slightly as he worked his penis in deeper and deeper. His hand jacked Adam's as he entered him.

Adam moaned with pleasure. "More, more." He pulled harder on his legs, opening wider for him. "Put it all in."

Gabe didn't need any encouragement. Adam's ass felt so good on his cock, he had to stick it in all the way. As his balls touched his hairy butt, he thought he would shoot his load, but he knew he had to hold back. Slowly, he pulled out, as he jacked Adam harder and faster. He plunged back in and lube sprayed out of his ass. He threw his head back as he entered him to the hilt. He held his cock in place, pressing on his prostate. He caused another wave of pre-cum to flow out of Adam. He added that to the lube and jacked him harder.

"Faster," Adam pleaded.

Gabe doubled his pace and made his balls slap his ass. Slap, slap, slap. Flesh hit flesh. He slammed into him harder and harder. The intensity increased, and he couldn't hold back any longer. He plowed into Adam as hard and as fast as he could. His hand worked his dick as fast as he plunged into him.

Adam never felt this before, he couldn't believe the pleasure. He lay back and thrust his pelvis at Gabe, moaning with each thrust. He felt the pressure grow and grow, and suddenly, he couldn't take it anymore. His cock exploded in Gabe's hand. Hot, white cum sprayed across his chest and face.

Gabe jacked his cock harder as another wave shot out of him. The warm goo set off his own orgasm, and he thrust onto him and filled his condom. His tip hit Adam's prostate and triggered another eruption. His hand filled with semen as it flowed between his fingers. He couldn't stop despite the overload of sensations in his body and in Adam's.

Adam begged him to stop, but Gabe couldn't. Another spasm hit and added to the condom. Adam's arms let go of his legs and grabbed his shoulders, "Stop, stop, STOP!"

But Gabe pulled almost out and thrust back in. He squeezed hard all the way to the tip and sent another orgasm between them. He leaned forward and collapsed on top of Adam, still buried deep inside his ass. They lay there in each other's arms, fluids and goo, oozing all over their bodies.

As his breathing returned to normal, he pulled out of Adam's ass.

Adam screamed with the release. He rolled onto his side, gasping.

Gabe spooned his body, which almost sent Adam back into orbit. He held onto him as they lay there, dripping.

Finally Gabe said, "Did you want to sauna and shower?"

Adam rolled onto his back, into a pool of cum.

Gabe stroked his cock and nibbled on his ear.

"I need one badly."

They stood on unsteady legs and shuffled over to the sauna. The stove was on, and the moist heat greeted them as they entered. Adam spoke freely in the sauna. He sat exposed and comfortable, no longer ashamed of his body or its responses.

Gabe told of his wrestling and promised to be there starting Monday to help his dad and Adam.

"So, are you … do you …" Adam started to ask.

"I'm single and looking. I would love to meet another wrestler, in great shape, hot ass, big cock." He rubbed his hairy leg against Adam's. "And one my dad approves of." He moved closer to Adam and kissed him, as he held his hot sweaty body against him.

Adam didn't mind.

# # # # #

Adam returned to the dorm and found Larry in bed, a naked leg hung over the edge of the bed. "Did Coach teach you a lot?" He scratched his belly under the sheets.

The room smelled of sex and male sweat. Adam felt his body respond and his dick became instantly hard. He licked his lips and smirked at Larry. "I learned a lot today, some interesting moves, and if you're good, I may even show them to you."

Larry pulled the sheets down a little, and his pubic hair came into sight. "I know you enjoy watching me as I strut around here bare-assed."

Adam come closer and looked down at him in the bed. "You think so?"

"I do, and I'm willing to bet my ass you can't pin me in ten seconds." He turned on his side and flashed his fuckable butt.

"Larry, you've been asking for this all semester." And, Adam   pounced.

HEAVIES
By Landon Dixon

Dixon's writing credits include many magazines, anthologies and story collections.

Jackson stepped off the bus into the cold driving rain. Wilton, deep in the coal mining region of the state, way deep in the minor hockey league system; deep enough to bury a man permanently if he wasn't careful, suffocate his dream of ever making it to the NHL.

Jackson was twenty-two years old, a huge, hulking man with the scars on his face and fists already as testament to how he played the game: tough; his role in the game: enforcer.

He grimaced, ran a big, square-knuckled hand through his bright blond hair, looking up at the leaden sky, then across the street at the dilapidated, barn-like structure that was the valley city's arena. He heaved his hockey bag up onto a broad shoulder, shuddered slightly then strode across the street, intent on making the team.

Boyd hit the deserted city limits and drove on through. There was no brass band and cheering fans there to greet him, like when he'd won the Stanley Cup as a late-season add-on one long decade earlier. There was just wet, black, winding asphalt and abandoned warehouses and mills, craggy rocks jutting out from the moon-like landscape. He shifted the GTO down, slowing, slowing, always slowing, headed down into the valley. From the pinnacle of pro sports to near absolute bottom.

Boyd was thirty years old, six feet tall, thickly muscular. His nose had been broken so many times it wandered his face, and his knuckles were so out of alignment they'd never form straight rows again no matter how many surgeries he had.

He drove through the flashing yellow intersection lights along Main Street, turned off, into the parking lot of the arena. Then he snapped off the rumble of one of the last remaining toys of the glory days. He stepped out into the rain, lugged his hockey bag out of the car's trunk, and stared at the eighty-year-old arena.

It had come down to this, his dream of reliving the triumph that he'd tasted far too early and far too easy. The steady slide down had seemed inevitable after that, fueled by booze and boredom and a belief in invincibility.

Boyd shuddered beneath his leather jacket, threw back his long black hair, a hard man still, but nowhere near unbeaten. His brown eyes shone with memories; and a fierce, renewed determination to give it one last shot. If he could latch on as the enforcer for the Thunder, he could begin the long climb back up. Anything beat driving a delivery truck for a living.

He caught movement out of the corner of his eye — a man walking across the street toward the arena; a big, broad, tough-looking man, striding confidently. Their burning eyes met through the pouring rain in the pre-dawn chill, and they both knew their jobs had just gotten a lot harder.

# # # # #

They tangled during the first practice. The coach of the Wilton Thunder was a white-haired, red-faced guy who had worshipped at the temple of Fred Shero many, many hockey moons ago. He watched with a twinkle in his milky eyes, as Jackson and Boyd dropped the gloves before a puck had even been dropped and circled each other.

They clutched uniforms, started throwing. A right bounced off Boyd's temple, a left drove into Jackson's nose. It went back and forth, punches thrown at a furious pace, some landing, most not. Until their uniforms were so tangled up and the pair so exhausted that they didn't protest when the coach yelled at two other players to break it up.

"I like the game played rough and tough!" Coach barked afterwards. "Team tough. There's only going to be room on this squad for one goon."

The die was cast.

The first shift of the first scrimmage, Jackson nailed Boyd into the boards with a cross-check. Boyd saw stars then came up swinging.

They bloodied each other's noses. Boyd's lower lip was split open down the middle. The coach let that fight go on for a full minute, the other players whacking the boards and the ice with their sticks when it was finally all over.

But it wasn't all over, not by a long shot. In the small, dreary dressing room afterwards, Jackson was bending over to pick up a roll of tape, dressed just in his jock, when Boyd shoved him from behind, headfirst into the row of metal lockers.

Boyd's upper body was bare, and his muscles popped all over his arms and chest, his smooth, pale skin gleaming with perspiration under the thirty watt bulbs. "That's for your cheap shot," he growled at Jackson.

The other picked himself up and gave his head a shake. His wet blond hair flopped over his eyes, and he slicked it back. His tall, tanned body was thick with vein-striated muscles, his thighs flared wickedly wide from a summer school of power skating. "You're going to get more of those before this camp is over, old-timer. If you can't take it, retire." Jackson grinned a clean row of teeth.

Boyd's tongue inadvertently sought out the gaps in his own dental work, as his eyes roamed over Jackson's lean, handsome face and young, hard body. Then he turned as if to go but leapt back into the fray, tackling Jackson and smashing the both of them into the lockers.

The men grappled, their semi-nude bodies pressing together, big muscles straining. Boyd head-butted Jackson, momentarily stunning the younger man. Then Jackson kneed Boyd in the groin, the older man's jock only partially absorbing the blow.

They rolled onto the floor, around on the chewn-up carpet, the other players in various stages of undress scrambling to get out of the way. "Save it for the motel room on the road, lovers!" Coach suddenly barked, putting a halt to the wrestling match.

He slapped his clipboard against his thigh. "We're playing the Turnberry Wildcats tomorrow night, in Turnberry. Everyone gets to play. For now. Be back at the arena at six tomorrow morning. It's a five-hour ride on the iron lung, boys, one-way."

The other players groaned.

Boyd and Jackson got to their feet, glaring at one another.

# # # # #

Jackson quickly discovered that he and Boyd were already sharing the same motel in Wilton, a horseshoe-shaped, two-storey structure along the highway on the west side of town. He was walking by the leaf-filled wreck of the swimming pool, headed for the ice machine to continue nursing his various bumps and bruises, when he spotted Boyd through the partially open door of Room 12. The older man was stretched out on his bed in his underwear, watching a black and white movie on TV. Despite the frigid temperature outside, the ancient, overheated rooms made cracking a door or window mandatory.

Jackson thought about just walking by. He thought again.

"Better get your beauty sleep, old-timer," he said, smacking Boyd's door wide open with his free hand.

Boyd leapt off his bed and into a fighting stance. Then he saw that Jackson was wearing just a bathrobe and flip-flops, an ice bucket in his hand, and he grinned at the man's battered face. "Soaking your head in a bucket, huh? That's where it belongs, all right."

Jackson entered the small, dingy room, walked up to Boyd. "Why don't you just call it quits right now, Pops? Save my knuckles some punishment."

Boyd spat in the man's face.

The hot spit struck Jackson on his left cheek, rolled down. He spat in Boyd's face, catching the other man full in the mouth.

Boyd licked Jackson's saliva from his lips, swallowed. Then he thumped the bright purple bruise on Jackson's chest, just above the man's left nipple. He didn't hit him hard with his folded fist, just enough for Jackson to really feel it.

The blond rocked back on his heels. He slapped Boyd's face, catching the smaller, stockier man right on the stitched-up cut that decorated his left cheek like a war ribbon.

Boyd's head twisted to the side, and he groaned. He put his hand up to finger the wound. Then he tore Jackson's bathrobe open, grabbed onto the man's semi-erect cock and gave it a twist.

"Fuck!" Jackson grunted, jumping up onto his toes, his cock swelling in Boyd's hot, gripping hand despite the pain. He dug his fingernails into either side of Boyd's underwear and ripped the skimpy white briefs down.

Boyd's cock flopped out into the open, huge and heavy with blood. Jackson grabbed onto it, roughly pulled it. Boyd gasped and jerked forward.

The men stared at one another, face-to-face, cocks clenched tightly in each other's hands, cocks growing hard as their bodies and thoughts. Jackson mashed his mouth down onto Boyd's mouth, savagely kissing the man. Boyd fought back with his tongue, shooting it into the younger man's wet open mouth and slamming it up against Jackson's tongue.

They wildly Frenched, their cheeks bulging with each other's tongues, their hands clasping and pulling on each other's cocks; their hard, fully-engorged cocks, filling the squeezing hands with pulsating meat.

Boyd pulled his head back and attacked one of Jackson's taut, tan nipples. He bit into the rubbery bud, pulled on it, stretching it almost right off the groaning man's chest. Jackson grabbed Boyd's big, hairy balls with his other hand and gave them a ruthless jerk. Boyd groaned, but didn't let go with his teeth.

Jackson tugged on Boyd's prick, twisted the man's sack. As Boyd left his teeth marks behind on Jackson's one nipple, swirled his wet, red tongue all around the other. The blond grunted and shivered, sticking out his muscle-humped chest, spearing his cock deeper into Boyd's hand.

Boyd grasped Jackson's blond-dusted balls and gouged them with his fingers, digging into the testicles, separating and squeezing them individually. As Jackson sunk his fingernails into the veiny shaft of Boyd's cock and scratched all along its rigid length. The men panted, straining against one another, their big, heated, naked bodies close together.

Then Boyd suddenly pulled his hand off Jackson's swollen prick and slammed the man on the side of the shoulder, sending him toppling over onto the bed. He quickly joined his teammate there, the two men wrapping into a

29

sideways sixty-nine, legs upraised for easy access to cocks and balls and asses.

Boyd inhaled Jackson's smooth, sculpted hood, sent his mouth and lips sailing down Jackson's clean-cut shaft. The blond followed suit, blossoming his red lips over Boyd's bloated cap and pouring his mouth down the brunette's bumpy shaft. The two men clutched at each other's muscular butt cheeks, joined at the mouth and cock.

Boyd moved his head back and forth, sucking Jackson's prick. He didn't go easy, though, giving the young man another rough ride, teeth scraping shaft, biting into hood. Jackson reciprocated, giving inches, and taking them, biting into Boyd's shaft, chewing on the man's cap.

The bed groaned with their heated movements, straining to contain the heavy pair of lusty he-men. The men sucked hard and fast on one another's cocks, cramming their mouths and throats full of throbbing meat, neither backing down from the challenge.

Boyd pulled his mouth off Jackson's cock only long enough to spit on two of his fingers, suck on the pair of digits. Then he swallowed the blond's pipe again, and hooked his slickened fingers in between Jackson's quivering butt cheeks and down into the man's asshole, busting pucker and plunging two knuckles deep.

Jackson groaned around Boyd's cock, his body jumping with the erotic intrusion of the fingers up his ass. He fought back with his own digits, rapidly wettening three and ramming them into Boyd's manhole.

The brunette gasped, gagging on Jackson's cock, the man's long fingers diving full-length into his chute. The two men shimmered all over, ablaze with emotion, cocks jammed deep into mouths, fingers plugged deep into asses. And then the fucking began.

Neither man would give ground in the battle for supremacy, in the bedroom as it was on the ice. So neither would allow the other to top him, stick cock in ass and fuck bottom. So they pumped their hips, and fingers, fucking one another's mouths and throats and asses.

Jackson churned Boyd's wet-cauldron of a mouth with his cock, as he slammed his fingers back and forth in Boyd's chute. And Boyd did the same, driving his dick into Jackson's mouth, fucking the man's face, as he hammered ass with his fingers, reaming Jackson's anus.

The temperature in the tiny, stifling room skyrocketed, the air thick and heavy with the funk of sex and sweat, the muffled groans of the two men fucking and getting fucked. Neither would let up, pumping mouths, pumping asses. Their bare bodies shone with perspiration, their big muscles straining, buttocks clenching.

On and on it went, cocks and fingers pistoning, throats and butts getting ravaged raw. Until, at last, Boyd jerked, Jackson jerked, the blistering sexual pressure built to the blow-off point, no stopping it.

Boyd exploded in Jackson's mouth, blasting white-hot semen down the man's throat, in fearsome rhythm to the fingers sawing his chute. His cry of ecstasy was drowned in a shooting sea of Jackson's sperm, the blond's cock rupturing in

Boyd's mouth and rocketing salty cum, Boyd's driving fingers spurring on the heady gouts of ecstasy.

The men shuddered and jetted and pumped and swallowed, over and over again. They blew out everything they had in their balls, even in their joy each trying to outdo the other in volume and intensity and repetition.

Finally, when the last tremors of all-out orgasm had rippled through their muscular bodies, they shifted around face-to-face on the bed. They kissed, giving back as good as they'd gotten, swirling each other's warm, rubbery sperm around in their mouths. They crossed tongues again in the gooey mess, their cocks pressed tight together like their bodies, clutching one another in their arms.

# # # # #

They fought the Turnberry Wildcats to a draw, Boyd and Jackson both scoring a pair of kayos. Then the two men fought each other in their motel bedroom that night, on the ice at practice the following day, after the long, exhausting bus ride back to Wilton.

A week in, even the jaded old coach was shaking his head in amazement. He'd never seen such consistent ferocity, a burning hatred so passionate. He wanted to keep both men, but the GM overruled him, trading Boyd away just before the start of the grinding eighty-four game minor league season — to a rival team in the same division.

The men fucked and sucked like wild animals in Jackson's motel room that night. Then Boyd jumped in his car and keyed the engine to life, roared off into the chilly, rain-streaked night with Jackson's warning that he'd kick his ass the next time they met — as opponents — ringing in his ears.

TAKE IT LIKE A MAN
By R. W. Clinger

R. W. Clinger writes for STARbooks Press. Of course, he accepts all sweaty, aggressive, and hot wrestlers inside his gym, among other confined places. Contact him at rwclinger@verizon.net or through his website, www.rwclinger.com.

ONE — TRICEPS AND TRIPLETS

Unconscious for two minutes …

"Seriously," I say in a rather robust manner, eyeing up the three beefcakes on the Champion mat inside Kick Him In The Basket, a gym on Edison Street specialized for kick boxing and the neighborhood muscle boys. "Let me get this straight. You want me to take all three of you meatheads on at the same time, right?"

Mo, Curly and Larry are prize kick boxers on the blue mat. Each is dressed in a pair of silver Rufskin workout shorts and nothing more. All three of the beefcakes nod and grin their handsome, jockish smiles in unison. The Sampson triplets are to die for, if you want to know the truth: bald with bright blue eyes, chests of steel, toned triceps, and twenty-seven years old. They stand at six-one, have humungous nipples that are golden brown, and sport pug-like noses that I simply find adorable. Rumor has it they are all queer as Tinker Bell and like to get it on with the same guy, and each other. Think Taboo or Taboo II all the way. It's just a rumor, though, which I doubt.

"Bring it," Mo says. "Nail us, bitch." He sounds dumb but cute as hell. All three of the Sampson brothers are like this. Muscleheads without IQs. Awesomely built houses without any furniture. Who really gives a fuck, though, since they are drop dead beefy and handsome, right? Honestly, it's worth closing the gym ten minutes early this evening just so I can fuck around with them on the mat.

I give them a crazy ass look and say, "What's in it for me, you three little pigs?"

Larry quickly pulls down the elastic rim of his silver Rufskin and shows off his uncut, six-inch long limp dick and its two friends in their loose and bald sack. "You get to blow us after we attempt to kill you."

"All three of you at the same time?" I question, intrigued with their naughty play.

"All three of us," Curly says.

I smile from ear to ear, rub my cock with my right hand, feel it jump to life, and become the happiest man in the world because three meaties are going to bash my skull in with their kick boxing skills and then take advantage of my mouth and throat with their cocks, one by one.

In truth, I've shared some heated sex with chiseled twins before. The Marco brothers were wild on the trampoline in my private gym. Both redheads used me up, spat me out, and came back for more … a dozen or more times after our first encounter. Sex with the twins was pretty amazing, but then again I'm not one to complain when I have a man at my front and his identical brother at my back, creating an edible sandwich out of me. That was three years ago, though. The twins unfortunately moved to Nebraska and fell in love with a cowboy, sharing the rustic dude. Both still live there with the rodeo champion. Now, I have the Sampson trio for my use, unable to complain and consider it a fair trade-up.

"We're ready, pretty boy," Mo informs, eyes up my Ryan Gossling looks, and licks his lips.

"Kill us," Larry adds, ready to pound me to the mat with his Herculean structure and dynamic alternating step-over front kicks.

"No blood," I say. "You know I faint at the site of it."

"We know," Curly says, rolling his eyes. "Now shut up and try to fuck us up."

What happens on the mat is tyranny, which I know is about to transpire because Trixie Snyde-Basket didn't raise a fool as a son. Curly does a left foot forward move on my chest and almost knocks the wind out of me. Mo carries out a center position kick, aims for my pecs, and nails me with some heat. Larry does a round house kick at my left shoulder and pushes me to the mat. The triplets give me enough time to stand up, shake my head, and let me say before they decide to annihilate me, "Pussies. You three can do better than that."

Mo says, "It's time to really fuck you up now, Mary Poppins," and giggles in a masculine manner. He does a rear-leg side step and then a lead-leg kick, which nails me in my right thigh and stings like a motherfucker.

Larry carries out a shuffle to the right, jabs his left leg forward, but I jump quickly out its way and it misses me. Following his attempted jab, I say, "Better luck next time, Strawberry Shortcake."

Curly snickers and says, "My turn, asshole," teasing me. He carries out a three-kick combination with his right leg and foot, and sends me plummeting to the mat.

Down for the count, I am left breathless, dizzy, and semi-unconscious on the Champion mat. I shake my head to the left and now to the right, and ask, "Toto, are we in Kansas?"

The triplets laugh down at me, pull me up and off the mat, and all say at the same time, "It's time for you payment, bud."

"I need some water … cock … water … I can't make up my mind."

"You're getting cock," Mo says and positions me on my knees.

All three guys push their Rufskins down and step out of the tight material.

Larry pries my mouth open with his cock-like thumbs and fingers.

Curly stands behind me and holds my head in position.

Mo smacks my cheeks with his deflated tool, which begins to grow into nine inches of hard fun.

"Eat it," Larry instructs, "Make Mo hard."

What transpires next is nothing I have ever accomplished before in my twenty-nine years. Mo directs his beef between my lips and slides the lengthy mass into my throat. He allows the tube of meat to grow into its full nine inches and begins to fuck my face. About a minute later, Larry does the same thing. Then Curly. All three of the brothers take turns on my mouth and build up their orgasms. Each plug my narrow breathing passageway with their tools, one by one, share a few bucks with my opening, pull out and away, and use my face as their homoerotic toy.

Of course, I gag and choke, murmur indecipherable words, and feel numb and confused because of their triple use with my mouth. Truth is I wouldn't have it any other way. Larry bangs my throat the hardest. Mo holds my head. Curly slaps his bald balls off my chin. Each become brisk regarding their individual motion, pound my head with swift motion, and plan to …

I come in my Diesel shorts without having my eight-inch cock touched, licked, or blown. Honestly, I do. The trio becomes so hot with their mouth-fucking that I can't keep my load pent for a second longer. Bubbles of cream explode from the hard shaft in my shorts and ooze covers my thighs, balls, and my pubic triangle. Stickiness soaks the material at my middle, and I become empty of my load, self-spent, but still into our athletic foursome.

"Let's cream him," Mo says to his brothers.

"I'm game," Larry says.

"Me, too," Curly adds.

All three of the steamy, hot, and sexual brothers instruct me to lie down on the mat and stare up at them. Mo stands between my legs and starts to crank the nine-inch stick of beef between his muscled legs. Larry is positioned at my left side and does the same thing. Curly stands on my right side and manipulates his spike with both hands.

Believe it or not the three brothers become synchronized with their handy motion. Bucks occur in unison, and their moans fill the empty gym after hours. Hands become wild on their solid shafts and rise and fall all at the same time. Perspiration builds on their sculpted chests and meaty thighs. The droplets fly off their skin and drizzle my suntanned body. Each kick boxer huffs and puffs, ready to blow his load.

Mo says, "Aim for his face."

Larry adds, "Don't spray it in his eyes."

Curly admits, "I'm going for his mouth."

How long do they manipulate their sticks? Seven … nine … eleven minutes, I'm really not sure, dizzy under their labor. Their movement is swift and concurrent, relentless and about as hot as hell. I calculate their hardy motion as Hot House-perfect and up to Colt standards. The trio is not at all shy about performing above me, and so very brazen regarding unloading their oozy man-spent all over my frame.

Within seconds I'm doused with their cream. White, sticky goo fires out of their spigots and floods over my chest. My dented navel, pumped pecs, and lined abs become goo-covered. Strings of spew nail every inch of my torso, and I obtain a glue-bath by the triplets. My corded neck and ripped shoulders are also splattered with their creamy substance. And helplessly, still beneath them, their Sampson splat sizzles against my skin, just the way they desire.

After all workouts at the gym, paying members can use the shower area and clean up. The three brothers are well aware of this perk and take advantage of it. In fact, they pull me off the Champion mat with their muscular arms, raise me above their Spartan bods, and carry me to the showers where I am rinsed under warm spray, washed down with soap and suds, and eventually rinsed, being cared for with their big palms, wide grins, light spanks, and pleasurable laughter.

TWO — UNDER HIS MUSCLES

Unconscious for five minutes …

No, our foursome after hours is not discussed among us. In fact, a few days pass, and the trio eventually arrives at my gym for a kick boxing workout. Here, they practice step-over front kicks, rear-leg side step kicks, and jumping front kicks. The threesome murder each other on one of the mats inside the gym and become quite the spectacle for a number of paying members.

During their vein-popping and sweaty workouts, my assistant, Kenford Ross, demands my attention in our shared office, so we can work on the agenda and schedule for the upcoming 3rd Annual Kick Boxing Championship, which is in three weeks. Two-hundred-seventy-two kick boxers have applied for the competition, some of which are locals to New York City, and others are from the tri-state area and beyond, but only twenty of the best will be chosen to compete. One of Kenford's jobs is simple: he has to watch videos of the hot and sweaty men in action on a seventy-inch flat-screen in the office and decide who will be the best competitors. Following his viewing pleasure of the chiseled athletes, he will notify the chosen kick boxers by phone, text, or e-mail, and tell the men that they have a chance at winning the twenty-five-thousand-dollar prize and an all-expenses-paid, five-day trip to Hot Springs, California.

Kenford looks like an adorable Mark Salling from Glee. The cutie has an ear-to-ear smile on his face and a pile of notes in front of him on the desk. Upon my entrance into the office, he says, "So far I have ten guys chosen for the competition."

"Forward me your notes in an e-mail and I'll get back to you."

His smile doesn't dissipate, which I find peculiar, since he is not the smiling type. "What's going on?" I question, and point at his grin.

"I can't tell you," he says, and shakes his head.

"I'm your boss, which means you have to tell me."

The office is cluttered with enough paperwork to build a bathhouse. Stacks of the shit lie around everywhere. Too many things are hidden and unfound in places, but neither Kenford nor I have any ambition to clean it up. Now, he points to the Pelco DVR player in the corner and says, "I reviewed the gym's security tape from the other evening. It looks like there was some after-hour activity."

I roll my eyes, shake my head, and know where his confession is heading. Obviously, he watched my blowjob performance on the triplets, and our shoot session together. "Don't even go there, young man."

"I thought about putting the sex scene on the Internet, but I didn't want to get fired."

"Good choice."

"But I must admit, it was crazy hot. I jerked off to it twice. You certainly know how to give a blowjob, man, especially to triplets."

I snap in his direction, point a finger at him, and say, "Knock it off, Kenford. Keep this professional. What happens in the gym stays in the gym. You know that."

He ignores me and laughs. "Of course."

"Of course," I reply, walk out of the office, blush with a smirk on my face, and seek out a few of the gym's members to teach a kick boxing class.

# # # # #

Mo Sampson desires my attention after the gym closes. He's the last one in the establishment, takes a long shower by himself, dries off, and searches me out inside the gym with nothing more than a cotton towel wrapped around his waist.

Kenford has already gone home, which leaves Mo and me alone among the boxing gloves, workout rings, boxing bags, various mats, weight stations, and kick boxing gear. He finds me next to the boxing ring. Spongy gloves are scattered over the floor because members haven't picked up after themselves. I'm in the process of tidying up the area when Mo steps up to me in his towel and says, "Can we talk about the competition coming up?"

I take in his chiseled body again: rounded pecs of iron, triceps from hell, comma-shaped navel, ripped stomach with no hair, and hard nipples. I nod and reply, "If you're worried about making the cut, you don't have to. You and your brothers are in the competition."

"Really?" he asks, blushing and happy at the same time.

"Yes," I say and nod. "Didn't Kenford tell the three of you?"

He shakes his head. "We had no idea."

"Maybe he plans on telling you tomorrow."

"Maybe. I'll wait and find out."

Now I expect him to walk away, get dressed, and leave for the night, but he doesn't. Instead, he simply stands in the same spot and shares, "There's something else I want to talk to you about, Basket."

"Ian," I say. "Call me Ian. My closest friends do."

"Thanks, I will."

"What do you want to talk about?"

He looks down at the mat around the boxing ring, which is gray, covered in footprints, and needs a good cleaning, which I make a mental note about. Mo clears his throat and admits, "I want some one-on-one with you, man."

I laugh, wonder why he looks embarrassed, and admit, "I'm always up for some kick boxing in the ring, Mo. You know that."

"Mark," he corrects me. "My name is Mark. Mo is my nickname. I want you to call me Mark, though."

And Curly's name is really Curt. And I hate to be called Basket, even if it's my last name. Truth is, I respect his correction and say his name. Now, I add, "I'm sorry, I get it."

He shakes his head and says, "It's not that kind of one-on-one I want with you." Before providing anything more, he drops the towel to the floor and shows off his rod for my desire. The thing is semi-hard and delicious looking. His balls swing underneath the piece of meat, which are probably ready to be licked, sucked, and played with. Calmly, he says, "I want some naked one-on-one with you, Ian. What do you think?"

I chuckle, greedy for his built bod, and find him sexy as hell and totally alluring. The man is Corbin Fisher or Chaos Men all the way. "Okay then," I say, "now that we have that confession out in the open."

He gives his wanker a tug, spins around, shows off his ass, and says, "I want you to fuck me, man. My ass wants your cock in the worst way. Are you up for the job?"

"Nice ass," I say, and visually absorb his rounded rump-cheeks, tight looking back, thick thighs, and its deep and erotic crease that designs his bottom. "In truth, I can fuck that if you want me to. All of you Sampson boys are my type."

He spins back around, grins at me, and says, "Fuck me in the middle of the boxing ring, here and now."

"Really?" I ask, a little surprised by his demand, and completely caught off guard by it. A blowjob is one thing, but a fuck-fest in the boxing ring is ... totally over the edge and explains his true attraction to me and my cock.

"Yes, really. And I don't want my brothers to know about it. I want to keep this our little secret."

I nod my head and reply, "I can do that. My lips are sealed."

"Your lips need to be on my ass," he confesses, chuckles, and surely feels at ease with my company now.

"Are you sure that you can handle my thick dick?"

"I'm a master at handling dicks like yours."

"If I plug your bottom with it, it's going to hurt. Are you up for that?"

"Don't fool yourself, Ian, it's why I'm here."

# # # # #

Not even five minutes later the Sampson triplet has me right where he wants me: naked inside the boxing ring, on my back, hard as a Cybex weight between my legs, and plastic over my shaft. Greedily, he faces me, spreads his legs, and lowers his asshole over my upright spike. One inch of my post enters his bottom, and he gasps like a little boy. The second inch causes a murmur of excitement to exit the man's lips. The third inch forces an aggressive moan out of the man. And half of my dick causes the beefy to lose his balance, almost roll off me, and plummet to the boxing ring's cushy mat. Five inches of my eight probe his insides with an extra push. Six inches prompt the athlete to generate a moan above me. Seven inches pulverize his asshole. And eight final inches buck inside the queer kick boxer, blast his tight hole with the finest entrance, and send him to a higher plateau of lust and euphoria.

Under his muscles, Mark decides to ride my two-inch-plus wide cock like a sexy hustler. Quick and jarring north and south motion occurs on the post. The gym buddy rises and falls, groans and moans with delight, and calls down to me, "Fuck me, Ian! … Fuck me hard!"

Frankly, he carries out all the work. The video created by the Pelco DVR mounted in the gym can prove such queer and intimate details. I merely lie still in the center of the boxing ring's mat while the jock rides my tool. Maybe one or two strikes to his muscular rump occurs, but honestly, this is about the extent of my physical action. Not that I'm complaining that he does all the work, of course.

His face is red, puffed, and looks streaked with sweat. He squints his eyes, moans above me again, and hangs on for the cock-ride by clamping his ass tightly around my post. His movement is wild atop me as he pleasures himself. The rider is brisk with his steady action. Again and again, he rises and falls on my tool, building his orgasm. One lift and fall turns into dozens, and he attempts to get off because of my eight inches that chaotically glide in and out of his core. Perspiration splashes my chest and … "Woof! … Woof! … Woof!" escapes his parted lips, which prove his state of elation and man-with-man delight. A rock waves between his legs and bounces against his taut navel, which he manhandles with his right palm and fingers.

Vibrant, feisty, and unyielding pleasure surfaces on the triplet's handsome face. His cheeks turn a fiery red and echoes of delight exit his mouth. His hand is in a state of overtime on his tool. Mark becomes uncontrollable with his labor, into his gig and our fun together. And after a fifteen-minute ride and hand job to himself, the jock calls out, "Blowing my load, man."

"Come," I instruct. "Do it. Let it loose. I'm also going to shoot my load."

Mark listens. As he rises up and down on my pole and toys with the meaty stick between his massive thighs, we erupt our loads at the same time. The stud fires his ooze against my plated chest and decorates my pumped skin. The sap clings to my bare flesh in various areas and accentuates my torso's definition in a queer manner, which I sort of get off on and enjoy.

I come quickly, bursting a condom-filled load into his tight ass.

Together we ride out our explosions, huff and puff, become spent, and …

# # # # #

He kisses me before he leaves for the night: passion-driven, tongue-sharing, and spine-numbing. Thereafter, he says something crazy like, "Look for my brothers. They're after your skin. They also want to feel your cock inside their rears."

"What are you talking about?" I ask, but Mark Sampson is already gone. He vanishes from my side, into the night … until we meet again, of course.

# # # # #

The following morning I wake up late and have to open the gym since Kenford is off for the day. I take a quick shower, dress in my regular gear, which consists of a Go Softwear teal tank, snug Diesel shorts, ankle-high socks, and a pair of Nike runners that match my tank. I make the 2.8-mile drive to the gym in my lime-colored Mustang, open the place up, accomplish some paperwork, pay a few bills, scan the company's e-mail, prepare the protein shake bar for the early risers who use the gym at breakfast, and head to the equipment room because I hear a strange grunting noise.

Once inside the room, which is filled with mats, workout balls, weight machines, and a variety of other sports equipment, I see Larry Sampson seated on a stack of multi-colored mats. The beefcake has his workout shorts pushed down to his ankles and his nine-inch erection stands upright at his middle. Creamy-white man-spurt is splotched all over his torso from his post-sex jack-fun.

I shut the office equipment room's door behind me in case early birds happen to walk into the gym for their workouts, seal us off from the rest of the waking world, and say, "What's this about, Larry?"

He feeds himself the morning goop that hangs from his left nipple, sucks a fingertip, pulls the digit out of his mouth, and admits, "It's an early workout for me. A few minutes earlier and you could have joined in on the fun. I would have let you blow me again if you wanted to. I think I would have liked that, and maybe you would have, too."

I roll my eyes and say, "You're brother said you'd be coming around."

"And coming between my legs, I hope," he snickers.

I don't know what to say to him. Half of me is pissed because of the scene I walk in on. The other half is stone-hard between my legs because of his sex-act on the spare mats and the creamy load that glazes his firm nipples and cut abs.

"Which brother?" he inquires, lapping up the morning chow from his chest.

"Mark."

"The frisky one of the three," he admits. "He's always in someone's pants. Mark has an unstoppable libido." He rolls another fingertip over his plated chest, lathers the tip with his ooze, and feeds himself. Following his snack, he asks, "Did Mark get with you?"

I keep quiet, still, and decide to let him accomplish all the talking. Why incriminate myself, right?

"He did get with you. I can see it in your eyes, Basket. When did it happen?"

"Last night," I break down and say. "In the boxing ring."

The triplet laughs and says, "He knows how to smooth talk the guys. Mark is a master at seduction. I should have warned you."

Enough. The guy needs to head to the showers, clean the gunk off his chest, and go home. I have work to do and a gym to run. After I tell him this, I say, "And mind your own business about my sex-gigs with Mark."

He stands, pulls up his shorts, and conceals his goods. Larry lets out a little laugh and says, "Trust me, it's hard to stay out of your business when my brothers are after your hot ass."

"What are you talking about?"

"Mark had you in the boxing ring and … my brother Curt is next. You wait and find out."

"You're crazy," I say. "Curt has better things to do than my ass."

"Trust me, pal, he digs your ass and wants it," he says, chuckles, and heads to the showers for clean-up from his post-jackoff session in the equipment room on the extra mats.

THREE — KICK ME WITH YOUR BEST SHOT

Unconscious for ten minutes …

The list of the twenty kick boxers who will be competing in the 3rd Annual Championship is posted in the gym. Larry, Mark, and Curt's names all appear on the bulletin board. The threesome are about as happy as queer virgins in gay strip club, high on an adrenaline buzz because of their fortunate news, and want to kill all the members' asses in a kick boxing gig on the mats before the competition.

To calm them down from their adrenaline rush, I decide to have a private meeting with them in the equipment closet at the gym. All three sit on the extra stack of mats and listen to my speech. "The three of you are gloating and need to stop it."

"It's our right to gloat," Larry says.

"It's not," I correct.

"We're just so excited to be in the competition," Mo admits.

"Keep some of your excitement under wraps. A lot of the gym's members didn't make it. Show them some respect. Don't be a bunch of assholes."

Mo gives me a seductive wink and says, "They didn't make it because they didn't fuck around with your cock and ass."

"Shut the fuck up, Mo!" I hiss, growing irritated.

"Mark," he corrects. "I told you to call me Mark."

"Whatever!" I bark at him. "Get your shit together and meet me on a mat. We'll argue this out with some prize-winning kicks. What do the three of you say?"

Curt says, "I haven't fucked around with your cock and ass yet, but I want to."

I shake my head in disgust, turn away, secretly smile regarding his confession, and head to the mats on the main floor for some classic ass kicking to the Sampson trio.

# # # # #

Less than five minutes later we stand on a mat together. The triplets are on one side and I'm all by myself on the other side. Frankly, I'm a person who prefers making love instead of war, but a little piece of me wants to kick their asses by using my professional fighting skills, just because they manage to piss off some of the gym's members.

Mo says to his brothers, "Kick it, boys," and all three men make a step forward, ready to down me on the Champion mat.

Girls run, but I'm not a girl. Gay guys on the other hand can battle with a smile, great hair, and enough power to take down the Spartans; this is exactly what I accomplish. In brief, growing up as a faggot sucked because of bullying, and all that rage seems to come to a head on the mat. An absorbent amount of power is discovered, and used, all within just a short period of time.

"Kick me with your best shot, boys," I say to the trio, who seem to transform into what look like a bunch of beefy, sweaty, and pretty boy serial killers on the opposite side of the mat.

Mo says, "Kill him, bros. Don't waste a second more."

Larry growls, "On it."

And Curly challenges, "Break all his bones."

I've had a few acting classes in my days just for the fun of it and use them now. I lift up my right hand, check out my fingernails, blow on them, act as if I file them with an invisible emery board, blow on them a second time, and now say, "Whatever."

The trio is pissed, ready for action, and assault me with their muscles and kick boxing skills. Mo executes a rear-leg front kick on me and lets out an aggressive grunt of power. Larry does an alternating windmill kick on my ass, and I love every second of it. Curly performs a boxer's shuffle forward and backward, and follows it up with an impressive lead-kick.

Truth is, I'm not a fool, and know they have me right where they want me. I'm not Chuck Norris, a Teenage Mutant Ninja Turtle, or Captain American, although most kick boxers want to be. I've taught the sexy brothers exactly what they use on me now, and feel proud of them as they apply their steady footsteps, lunges, and combination kicks. No wonder they are in the top twenty kick boxers in the tri-state area division, ready for the upcoming competition and a solid win among the three of them.

Yes, I give it my best on the mat. Front kicks are used, lead-leg kicks are shared, and a trio of cross cuts with my right leg are textbook perfect. I'm a professional and prove such on the mat, but this doesn't mean I beat them. In fact, the opposite occurs. Mo gets me good after he huffs, "Kick him in the basket." The guy applies a solid front-lunge-kick to my left hip and I'm down for the count, feel pain arch through my side, and …

FOUR — WHY ARE YOU DUDES NAKED?

Conscious now …

"Ian, are you alright? … Can you hear me, man?" Curt asks above me. I blink a few times, look into his handsome blue-blue eyes, and feel his fingers and one of his palms on the left side of my face. Over his right shoulder is not my gym. Instead, I see parts of his studio apartment on Ross Street: Ikea furniture, naughty DVD collection on a cheap looking bookshelf, his goldfish Alejandro in a bowl on the kitchen table, and a Hot House 2014 calendar on the wall. My view shifts back to the pretty boy muscle head positioned above me. He's on his knees next to me and his dick is semi-hard between his beefy legs. The shaft is decorated with a bubble of ooze at its tip and drips to the oak floor.

"What happened?" I ask, feel my head spin, see two of Curt, now one again, and believe I'm going to throw up because my stomach is a little off-kilter.

"We were wrestling on my bed, making out, and … you fell off. You cracked your head off the floor, man."

"I did?"

"You did."

"Fuck me," I say, and rub my left temple.

"I was trying to do that when you fell," he shares, giggling a bit.

"Why am I in your apartment?" I ask.

"You wanted to give me a private workout before the big kick boxing competition tomorrow. You said some man-fun between us would be healthy for me."

"How long have I been unconscious?"

"Ten minutes. I called 911. An ambulance will be here in …"

I find the strength to sit up and kiss him. My mouth meets his mouth and my left palm finds the rod between his legs, which I provide with a generous stroke. It's a kiss from hell with much potency and lust, which knocks the wind out of him a touch. And after the kiss, I instruct him, "Cancel 911. I'm fine. I'd rather fuck around with you instead of going to the hospital. Kick boxers are much hotter than doctors."

Distracting us, the door to his apartment bursts open and in walks his two identical brothers. Our attention is drawn to the intruding duo.

Mo hurriedly says, "We came as fast as we could … What happened?"

Larry asks with a bit of surprise in his voice, "Why are you dudes naked?"

I feel a fresh boner between my legs, push my dizzy spell and stomachache away, lean into the chiseled kick boxer above me, grin from ear to ear in a devilish manner, and simply whisper, "Tell your brothers to join us, Curt … Let's have our own championship of sex tonight. We'll have the time of our lives."

WRESTLING IN THE CLOSET
By Aiden Lovely

Aiden Lovely resides in New Hampshire. Lovely is a freelance writer, and his work has appeared in many anthologies. Contact him at chaserbane@gmail.com.

Chancer was cleaning out the closet when his boyfriend of two years, Gaston, appeared beside him with a big box in his hands.

"I'm really going to miss this place," he said.

Chancer looked at him, "I know. Me, too, but y'know, we could always renew the lease."

Gaston's shook his head, "Don't bother. Where we're going is much nicer."

Chancer then turned to the closet. It was amazing how much stuff accumulated since their time there. Their apartment was a wooden box located on the second floor of the duplex. He was going to miss this place. So many memories, but it was a small space, crowded with stuff he bought when they first moved in. It wasn't their first place; but it was the first one that they financed on their own. It was Chancer's idea to live like that. He romanticized the idea of living off funds they generated as a couple instead of using money from their parents. Gaston agreed with him. Chancer wanted to prove a point. In fact, it was because his parents didn't think he could manage with his boyfriend, he felt compelled to do it. They were moving on to bigger and better things like a nicer apartment located in Manhattan, which was more convenient for Gaston's work.

As he began to see the closet's floor, he spotted a spandex like top peeking out from behind a shoebox. He grabbed the stretchy blue attire and gave it a little tug. He then revealed a medium sized wrestling singlet. He examined it. The singlet carried a faint odor of sweat. He wrinkled his nose a bit. It definitely wasn't his, but he'd never imagined Gaston owned it. He then noticed a second one. He examined that one as well. He assumed he knew almost everything about Gaston, so why didn't he know about this?

He leaned his head back and from where he sat with his knees bent, his thin calves pressed against his thighs, he saw the busy Gaston boxing up books in the next room.

"Gaston," he called out, "Can you come here for a minute?"

"What is it?"

"You just need to come here. It's important."

Gaston appeared in the doorway.

"What is this?" Chancer said as he held up the singlet. A small smile welled up on Gaston's lips. He blushed, "Errr … I used to wrestle. Those are the singlets I used to wear." He ran his fingers through his hair. "I thought I told you," his words followed.

"Well … you didn't," Chancer said, "I just never thought you were involved in any sports back in college, especially not wrestling."

"There are a lot of things you don't know about me," Gaston said with a smirk. Chancer stared into his eyes from the floor.

"Like …?"

"Really, it's nothing. Drop it."

"What? Why?"

Chancer pursued the situation. Since Gaston was so wishy-washy about it, he was determined to get a confession. If Gaston could keep this from him, what else was he keeping from him?

Gaston stretched the fabric back and forth before he continued speaking, "Well, it's my old singlet from sophomore year of university. Amateur wrestling. I always wanted to wrestle in high school, but never got the chance, so I joined the wrestling team in university."

"So … you saved old singlets for what reason?"

Usually Chancer wasn't the type to give Gaston a hard time about something so trivial. The way Gaston reacted to the situation made him suspicious. Gaston really didn't seem like the type to wrestle even back in university. He was always a tall and slender man whom people described as wimpy. Gaston then walked back into the other room.

"Are you keeping this? Chancer?" he called out, holding a tacky vase. He waited a few moments. He knew Chancer could hear him, so the late response irritated him. He repeated himself, but still didn't receive a response. He then entered the bedroom.

Standing at about five feet, seven inches with choppy locks of brown hair and eyes so blue that his sockets cupped them like bathwater was Chancer dressed in the singlet. The red spandex gripped his long torso and stopped on his thighs. It clung to his slender muscles and revealed his smooth, pale chest.

"It's a little tight," he said. His cock protruded through the material. It was almost uncomfortable, but the way Gaston's eyes ogled him aroused him.

"It … looks good on you."

"You say that like it's not true," Chancer commented. He looked into Gaston's disgruntled face and said, "What's the matter? I know it's a little tight, but it's not too bad."

Gaston shook his head and then locked eyes with Chancer again, "You're not going to let this go, are you?"

Chancer answered with a lusty smirk. Soon they were both dressed in singlets, standing across from one another in their bedroom.

"You don't look too bad in that," Chancer said. The singlet wrapped around Gaston's lean body. The fabric hugged his bubble butt. Just seeing his boyfriend dressed like this was making Chancer's cock stir. He never knew amateur wrestling was this hot. Gaston pulled at the material, "I'm definitely much bigger now than I was in college."

"You mean your dick or …?" Chancer teased.

The fabric was squeezing Gaston's thick cock to the point where it almost looked painful.

"It doesn't feel as tight as it looks," he said with a smile, "Can you believe this used to fit me in college? I guess I'm a little more muscular than I was back then." He pulled at the attire again.

"Wrestle me. Show me some moves," Chancer said.

Gaston hesitated. The only thing he really remembered about wrestling was trying not to get hard when he was tangled up with another young man on the mat. The scene of his boyfriend across from him, dressed in an old sweat-smelling singlet, was quite sexy in its own. To say Gaston had a wrestling fantasy was accurate. He always did. It was his real motivation to join the wrestling team in university. When he was a teenager, he masturbated to the muscular guys tussling with each other on television.

"It's no fun if you're not fighting back," Chancer said as he pranced around Gaston with his back arched forward.

Gaston dodged Chancer's hands. He never thought he'd wrestle Chancer in their bedroom. Chancer's fingertips swiped at Gaston's shoulders. Gaston then darted at Chancer's legs. He grabbed Chancer's knees as the two crumbled to the floor. Even with Chancer's arms thrashing, he managed to dunk Chancer over his head. Chancer's thighs rested on Gaston's shoulders, and his balls pressed against Gaston's face.

"I could suck your dick in this position," Gaston joked.

"Maybe you should," Chancer's voice weaseled out from behind.

Chancer placed his palms on the carpet to block his face from touching it. He didn't expect Gaston to be so good at this. He struggled out of the position. He wiggled on to his stomach as Gaston flopped on top of him, applying all the weight of his body on his boyfriend. Gaston pinned the struggling Chancer from the back on the carpet.

"Well, this position seems so familiar," Chancer teased.

"Are you trying to make me hard?" Gaston replied.

Chancer rolled Gaston over using his shoulders, "I'm trying to distract you."

The two were then intertwined; each one anxious to pin the other. They tussled on the carpet. Gaston pinned Chancer several times. It was Chancer's lack of skill that put him at odds. He was smaller in height and stature, but that wasn't an excuse for his skills. The scent of sweat brewed from the movement. The combat was almost no different than their routine in bed. His blazing touch on Chancer's waist provoked so much sexual tension. With Gaston so close, breathing heavily, Chancer wanted to caress his body.

"It's harder to wrestle you because we're not padded with cups. I don't wanna hurt you."

"Oh so that's your excuse for lack of skill," Gaston taunted. He smirked. He then readjusted his singlet.

"I'm just letting you win."

"Oh, really? Then show me what you got."

Chancer stood across from Gaston again.

"Ready?" he said.

"Ready when you are," Gaston said.

Gaston then swiped at the young man. Chancer dodged Gaston's attempts to grab him. He lashed out and grabbed on to Gaston's shoulders. He yanked his boyfriend forward and that was when Gaston gripped Chancer's waist. A groan escaped Chancer's mouth. Gaston's force was much more than he imagined. Chancer fell on his back as he struggled for freedom. He managed to roll onto his side to avoid Gaston's pinning technique. He crawled on his hands and knees to escape, but Gaston got him in a headlock. Chancer's movement became staggered from the strength. He wiggled, but it was no use. The carpet felt hard against his flesh. The more he attempted to move, the more Gaston secured his grip on him. The attire made him a little slippery to hold down. Gaston then mounted him on the floor. His cock brushed against the crack of Chancer's ass.

"See I told you I was good," Gaston said as he tighten his headlock.

"Ow, ow, ow. You're hurting me," Chancer cried out.

"I'm sorry. Chancer, you ok?" He released his grip, rose up and then Chancer threw him over using his back. He rolled on top of Gaston and pinned his arms above his head.

They lay symmetrically on the carpet; Chancer on top of Gaston, their chests pressed together. With his face close to his, Chancer said, "Gotcha."

His breath tickled Gaston's stubble. His skin was hot and a little sticky.

"You little cheater," Gaston said as Chancer loosened his grip on his arms. They were silent, engulfed in a gaze. It had been a while since they were that close in a position like that. All the stress they endured lately distracted their love life. Gaston was busy with work so most nights, right after eating dinner, he'd fall asleep. Chancer on the other hand, coped with his boyfriend's exhaustion by masturbating.

Their chests heaved up and down. The symphony of his breathing harmonized with his boyfriend's; the air shifting in his pipes. At first, he flinched when the big hand brushed a strand of hair out of his face. He felt the other hand slink across his smooth waist. They were so close, the tip of Chancer's nose hovered above Gaston's. His hard-on confessed his feelings without the need of any words. His eyes remained locked on his lover's. His eyelashes fluttered in the silence. The aroma of sweat mixed with faint cologne washed over him. When was the last time he felt his man's touch in this way? The question glided through his mind. It had been too long. He missed this. He missed the natural scent. He missed the warmth. He missed everything.

"Gaston," the name unconsciously spilled from between his lips. He was now still like a painting, barely breathing — taking in the image of his man staring back at him. Gaston's hair seemed so black, and his skin was sun kissed. The smile curling from the corners of his lips was sweet enough to substitute a candy-cane. It was these small details that meant so much at this moment. He forgot how amazing it felt to know he was the reason for that smile on Gaston's face. If it were ever beaming at someone else the same way it was beamed at him, it would create a wound so deep, it'd never heal.

His heart pounded against his chest so hard, he imagined the noise was echoing in Gaston's ears. He then pressed his lips against Gaston's. It was a tiny kiss; just a brush of the groove of his lower lip. When he drew back, he felt a vibration in the spot where they touched. He kissed Gaston again. This time Gaston's arms wrapped around his shoulders and engulfed him in a deep kiss. His desires were more than obvious now.

Passion ran through his body as he navigated his tongue into his boyfriend's mouth. The jolting sensation stung the moist muscle when it collided with Gaston's. He flinched, and Gaston's embrace tightened.

Gaston's tongue lashed out at his. It coiled around Chancer's tongue, overlapping and pinning it down. Their tongues performed a sensual ballet. A hoarse moan pulled from Chancer's throat. The smacking noise from their lips touching crowded their ears. It was like a gentle wrestling match; their tongues intermingled. Saliva crawled from the corner of Chancer's mouth as he exchanged another kiss.

Their singlets layered the carpet in different positions. Chancer's body was as bare as the day he was born. Gaston was naked, too. He scattered small kisses along the imprint of where the singlet had pressed on Chancer's smooth skin.

"I love you," Chancer said with his fingers crawling on Gaston's back. His voice was so soft he could barely hear his own words. Gaston looked at him. His lips trailed along his waist once more. His thick black hair fell on the torso and mopped over Chancer's skin. It tickled but felt so cool. He played with Gaston's hair as he moaned. The fine locks weaseled through his fingers as the sensation welled up in his body. His fingers stroked the nape of Gaston's neck. The feeling of those soft lips pressed against his flesh made him flinch. He felt the warm breaths play tag with his pelvis. He giggled. It was funny how much the play wrestling stirred up their passion.

He lay docile on the mattress as Gaston caressed his canvas. Gaston kissed Chancer's penis. It was a soft kiss as he made his way upward. He kissed the young man's navel then planted kisses all the way up the torso. He stopped when he reached the chest. It was as if he wanted to admire Chancer's pink buds. His nipples yearned for attention.

"Take me," Chancer wanted to say. He held back. Gaston had only used his tongue on him, but already he felt as if he was ready to burst. He paced himself, anxious for the nipple play that awaited him.

Gaston's tongue hovered over the right nipple. The wet muscle was poised. The first touch caused a raging moan to escape Chancer. He tilted his head back. His brown hair scattered in chunks on the pillowcase. He flinched. The tongue massaged the nipple, coating it in layers of saliva. As that sensation began to die out, he then felt a new touch on the opposite side. Gaston's fingers were toying with the other one. He jerked. He was reaching his limit, but his body hungered for more.

Gaston pinched the nipple and simultaneously bit the other one. Chancer jerked at the new wave of pleasure overwhelming him. From the way Gaston massaged his skin, he felt his insides quiver. The sensual touch crowded his soft buds, plucking them until a vibrant heat could be felt through the tiny areola.

He trembled as Gaston kissed his collarbone. When the hot mouth connected with his neck, he lost control of himself. He was taken away in a sea of pleasure, drifting off into only a place Gaston could take him. His arms draped around Gaston's shoulders. He felt the man's warm breath on his throat. A soft murmur poured from between his lips. The pleasure manipulated his body. Gaston nuzzled his neck; kissing his jawline every so often. His lips moved in a scrunching motion, the tip of his tongue moving like fingers on the keys of a piano. He was engulfed in a frenzy of kisses.

"Take me now," he managed to say. As he attempted to repeat himself, Gaston's tongue then lashed out at his. Once again, his mouth was entangled in a wrestling match. The song of their lips smacking together filled the room. The renewed coolness of the pillow felt relieving against his skin. When their lips parted, he attempted to catch his breath, but only to have it stolen away in the same second. They locked eyes as their passionate kiss tapered off into small caresses.

Gaston paused for a moment. His eyes locked on Chancer's. The smell of sweat and love was so potent now. Chancer inhaled sharply. Their jagged breaths were loud. He leaned up, kissed his boyfriend and then retreated to his pillow. The smile left on his face was a mixture of challenge and seduction. His lascivious eyes pulled Gaston in like chains. His member was throbbing and swollen, yearning for release. He bucked his hips as if to bait Gaston.

"If you want to screw me, you have to pin me first."

His words massaged Gaston's ears. His tone was feisty and full of lust. He pushed on Gaston's chest, struggling to get the man down. His hands then moved to Gaston's shoulders. Gaston pulled back, causing Chancer to fall on top of him. He then rolled Chancer underneath him. This massive strength was unexpected. Chancer knew no matter the outcome, he'd let Gaston have his way with his body though. He scrambled to the floor to escape. Gaston followed him. He could barely keep his grip on the wiggling Chancer. The young man bucked, but when Gaston restrained him by the ankles, his penis flopped and his anus was briefly seen. His mounds of pale flesh bounced with his moment as well. He thrashed his legs; Gaston holding on to his ankles, slowing him down. Chancer struggled to crawl over the carpet. The bristles scraped against his knees. Gaston's grip loosened. In an attempt to pin him, he allowed Chancer to turn over. Chancer now lay on his back, breathing heavily. Gaston paused before he made his next move. He then sprang into action, lunging on top of him.

With Chancer underneath him this time, he held Chancer's wrists. He pulled Chancer's arms above his head. The young man wiggled his wrists, but he was no match for Gaston. He was helpless. Every aspect of his body was exposed. A bead of sweat rolled off Gaston's forehead and landed on Chancer's nose.

"I pinned you," Gaston whispered and then licked his lips as he leaned in. He pressed his sweet lips against Chancer's. They shared light kisses until Chancer parted his lips. He allowed the wet muscle to fill his mouth. His teeth scraped the tongue as it entered. A string of saliva connected them now. When it broke, Gaston pressed his tongue against Chancer's again. The young man closed his eyes as if he were being lulled away. The passion engulfed his body. He then wrapped his legs around Gaston's waist, his ankles loosely crossed. This was more than an invitation — it was a demand.

Gaston's breaths landed on Chancer's bare body as he coated his cock in lube. His slender muscles were now bugling. His cock was throbbing. It felt hot and hard against the quivering anus. Chancer trembled from his anticipation.

Gaston used his fingers first. He shoved one all the way inside. Chancer twitched. It wasn't until the second finger pushed inside that a groan slipped out of his mouth. He pulled both fingers out and then pushed them back in. The anus became dilated and drenched in lube. He motioned his fingers back and forth, enjoying Chancer's squeals. It was true that he seemed more sensitive to Gaston's touch than usually. He blamed the foreplay for his sensitivity. Gaston then moved his fingers as if they were scissors. He pulled his fingers out when he noticed the shuddering Chancer's cock, ready to gush any minute. If Chancer was already reaching his climax from just his fingers, Chancer would probably cum as soon as he rammed his cock inside.

Gaston then replaced his fingers with his cock. The hard meat pushed on the entrance. A new feeling entered Chancer's body. The tip slipped inside, but Gaston pulled it out. He teased the man underneath him.

Chancer lay now with his knees bent and his calves near Gaston's shoulders. His anus was begging. Gaston's cock penetrated the sensitive hole. Each inch that pushed inside was followed by Chancer's moaning. His voice was growing hoarse, but he couldn't hold back. His anus stretched farther to take in the mass. He squealed from the burning sensation of his anus consuming the meat. Gaston hesitated before he moved. He massaged Chancer's chest as he said:

"Are you ready for me?"

Chancer couldn't manage words. His face twisted in pain. He gave a head nod. The fiery meat inside throbbed as it probed him. Striking his pleasure spot, his fingers gripped what little piece of the carpet he could. His teeth were clinched together. He then bit his bottom lip to fight back his moans, and instead they came out as short hums. His toes curled as the penis touched his pleasure spot again. Gaston always did have a way of handling his body like no other man. His anus squeezed the meaty instrument. He was so tight. A groan tore from between Gaston's lips. He rocked back and forth. His cock was buried deep inside the man. It felt so good. It was as if their bodies were melting together. The rocking sent jolts of pleasure through Chancer's body. Gaston was devouring him — enjoying him through their passionate dance.

Chancer cooed as their pace quickened. He wanted to say "I love you," but instead, he could only manage to wrap his arms around his man.

Gaston's hands then massaged Chancer's shaft as his balls slapped against the flesh. His thrusts were strong. Chancer didn't know how much longer he could hold back. His cock was so hard — ready to release. He felt Gaston reaching his limit as well. The noise of their friction outweighed the sound of everything else.

Gaston's sweat was like diamonds running down his skin. His hair was now damp. His thrusts became harder and faster. His fingers handled Chancer's cock roughly. His hand slid up and down the shaft. The sensation swirled around in Chancer's body. He was ready to give in any second. A bead of sperm crawled from the tip of his cock. When Gaston stroked his cock again, Chancer couldn't hold back any longer. Feeling the throbbing muscle inside him at its limit as well, Chancer cried out as his cum gushed out like milk all over his abdomen. Simultaneously, Gaston grunted and filled his boyfriend with his jizz. He heaved a heavy breath and then slumped over onto Chancer. Chancer was breathing heavily as well. His hair stuck to his forehead.

They lay in silence; each trying to catch their breath.

"I love you," Chancer said after a while. His words poured out in chunks.

Gaston said nothing. He rolled beside his lover on the floor. Their fingers were intertwined. The odor from when their bodies were joined polluted the room. It felt so good to be that close to Gaston.

"I love you, too," Gaston finally said.

He wrapped his arms around the young man's frame and kissed him. It was a tiny kiss, but the feeling of their skin brushing together enveloped a new sensation inside Chancer. Gaston suddenly felt as if he could go again. His cock began to stir. Even he was surprised with his own stamina. He leaned upward and placed Chancer's hand on his now hard cock.

"Ready to go again?"

"What is with you tonight?" Chancer said with a small grin.

"I never told anyone but I've always had a fetish for wrestling. When I would see my friends dressed in singlets, I'd get so horny. If it wasn't for the cup, everyone could have seen my boner."

"Why didn't you tell me this before?"

"I don't know. I thought you'd think it was silly or barbaric."

"Well, you obviously don't know me as well as you thought you did."

"What do you mean?" Gaston made a puzzled face.

"I mean there's nothing silly about getting off on wrestling. Two half naked men entangled on a mat turns me on so much," Chancer licked his lips. He was also ready for more action. His anus was loose from the first round.

"That explained the old singlets," Chancer wanted to say. The singlets were even sexier to Chancer when he imagined the fabric clinging to the bare Gaston. They exchanged a few more kisses. The two became joined again by the cock and the anus as they wrestled until the sun played as their referee to bring in the new morning.

DRAGON, SLAYED
By Fox Lee

Fox Lee has appeared in several erotic gay anthologies. Her dog Joey Boy brags about this constantly at doggy daycare. https://www.facebook.com/fox.lee.3956?fref=ts

Ko didn't know what he expected from his last night in the ring. A sense of closure, maybe? Instead, when it was over, he felt like a loose kite being taken away by the wind. He used to be the Lunatic Dragon, a wrestler with no fear or common sense, who attacked opponents with no regard for his own body. The Japanese audiences loved him, and there was talk of interest from America. Now, he was just Ko again. All because of a condition found by chance.

The other wrestlers wanted to take him out for drinks after the event, but Ko talked his way out of it. The wrestlers needed their sleep; tomorrow would be another day in another prefecture. Not that it ever stopped any of them from drinking the night away. Wrestling was family, and drinking with his brothers was like breathing to Ko. Necessary for life, he thought. Hopefully he was wrong. Or better yet, let the doctors be wrong.

He told himself it wasn't that bad. His wrestling career was over, but his life was in no danger. Ko would have a long normal life, as long as he stayed away from aggressive pursuits. It was lucky that they found the back condition before he paralyzed himself. He didn't feel lucky. He felt like the victim of a cruel joke. All his life, Ko wanted to be a wrestler. He was given physical ability, charisma, and the chance to prove himself. He was good at his dream. When he walked out to the ring, his adrenaline raced; it didn't matter if it was a handful of people or a full crowd. He was the Lunatic Dragon; no one was better than him.

The wrestling organization had been careful not to put him in any danger for his send-off. The script was clever, involving a deal in which another wrestler lost his wife to the current villain. In order to get his friend's wife back, Ko, the most popular good guy, had to retire from wrestling. The fans were moved, and rumor had it they expected Ko to find some loophole and make a comeback — something else to feel guilty about.

The stadium had a janitor's closet in the men's locker room. When Ko's match was over, he snuck in and hid out for the remainder of the night. He listened to the familiar sounds he had taken for granted, like the way the lockers and showers created their own clumsy music. He could smell sweat, knowing how it made everyone's uniform cling to their bodies after a match.

At least that was one problem out of the way; his secret was safe. The one thing he had worried about. Deep down, Ko didn't think the organization would have shunned him for being gay, but he had been too much of a coward to find out. Maybe after some time passed, if it came up in conversation with his old friends, he would confess. It wasn't as if he had feelings for any of them.

Ko wasn't attracted to his own body type. He admired it, wouldn't kick it out of bed if it had a good personality attached, but his preference ran to smaller men. Plenty of time to chase them now, but what would his pick up line be? Ko had no idea what he was going to do for money. He never went to college and gave his whole adult life to wrestling. His father told him to come home and work for his brothers. Ko would rather cut his dick off and use it as bait.

After a while, the locker room was silent, and Ko knew everyone was gone. He walked into the open and went to the massage table, where he was stretched out before his match, and got on it. The soft surface compressed under his weight, and brought back memories. Ko tried to think about his future, but nothing came to mind.

"Ko?"

He recognized the voice of the organization's sports therapist. His real name was long and hard to pronounce, so from day one, he told everyone to call him Kitty. He hadn't been there that day, which Ko found strange until someone told him Kitty got another job, one where he didn't have to be on the road all the time, tending to men who brutalized their own bodies.

"What are you doing here?" Ko asked.

"I was in the audience. I waited for you to come out and started to worry. I missed you."

Kitty's Thai accent wove itself into his Japanese. He had been raised in Thailand, where he got his degree in sports medicine before being recruited to Japan. He was about Ko's height, but lean and absent the muscles that were the trademark of professional wrestling. He did have very strong arms and hands, as Ko could personally testify to.

"What were you doing in the crowd?" Ko asked.

"I don't work here anymore; I can't be in the locker room whenever I want."

"I mean, why did you come at all? I thought you got a new job."

"It was your big night. You think I would stay away?" Kitty came to the table. "Are you in pain?"

"No. I just wanted to think about things."

"You want me to loosen you up?"

"I barely fought."

"You're depressed. That does horrible things to the body. Consider this my goodbye present."

Ko smiled. Kitty had that affect on the wrestlers. He was gentle, soft spoken and knew how to get big, macho men to admit where they hurt and let him heal them. Ko saw him out of work once, walking with friends through Kabukicho. Kitty was drunk, laughing and having a great time. Ko had a pang of jealousy that night. He only knew Kitty as a professional, who kept his distance from the wrestlers after work and never drank when there was a show the next day.

"Take off your clothes," Kitty said.

"Why?"

"So I can get into your muscles. Usually you're wearing spandex, this is no good." Kitty pulled on Ko's jeans.

Ko jumped off the table and stripped down.

"Underwear, too," Kitty said. "I hate when my fingers get caught in them."

"I thought this was my present?" Ko asked. "Why are you the one giving the orders?"

He brushed away his uneasiness. He understood how briefs were annoying, given how much of his body Kitty was used to massaging. Maybe he should have kept his Lunatic Dragon outfit on. Kitty gave him a towel to cover his groin, and told Ko to lie on his back. He started with Ko's arms, and Ko gave himself over to the sensations of being massaged.

"What happened?" Kitty asked. "I mean, no one will talk about it. Or they don't know."

"I have a back problem. It doesn't hurt, but it makes it much easier to get hurt in a job like this."

"Do you get a lot of back pain?"

"None. I was surprised there was anything wrong."

"You were lucky. I know you don't feel that way, but you could have gotten hurt really bad."

"I know. I still wish they never found it."

"Idiot." Kitty massaged Ko's fingers one at a time. "What you mean is that you wish you didn't have the back condition."

Ko's eyes teared. He hoped Kitty didn't see them.

"This was my dream."

"A guy like you will have lots of dreams. You have too much energy to just sit at home."

"You think?"

It was the first time someone said anything like that. Everyone else felt sorry for Ko and avoided talking about the future.

"I didn't go to college," Ko said. "I have no degree, no passion for anything."

"You'll find something. Hang out with me. I know lots of weird people. You'll get ideas."

"Yeah? You want to go drinking in Kabukicho?"

Kitty paused, and Ko's heart stopped. Then Kitty laughed.

"You saw me one night? Why didn't you say hello?"

"You were busy."

"Being drunk isn't busy. You would love me drunk."

Kitty moved on to Ko's legs, kneading the muscles in his thighs to jelly before going down to his feet. Kitty was a magician with feet. They were, he said, the most important part of the body.

"Turn over," he told Ko.

Ko turned onto his stomach, and Kitty pulled the towel off. Ko protested, not sure why it mattered so much to him. Kitty had seen everyone naked; it was part of being in the locker room.

"I can't see your butt?" Kitty asked.

"I might fart."

"You won't be the first," Kitty said. "Massage releases all kinds of energy."

Ko couldn't imagine farting on Kitty and being able to face him again.

"Anyone I know?" He asked.

"Yes. But I won't say who. Not that they would care, I hear all about the pranks you pull on each other."

"That's different, this is your job. Where are you going, anyway?"

"Sports medicine clinic in Tokyo. We'll be neighbors."

"Until I get evicted."

"If you get kicked out, I'll visit you in Ueno park."

Ko was going to call him a bad word, but Kitty was at the small of his back, and Ko was in too much bliss. When there wasn't an ounce of stress left, Kitty's hands moved on and surfed over his butt-cheeks. Ko moaned and pressed into them.

"Sorry," he said. "I didn't mean to do that."

"It's OK; you're supposed to like it."

I'm not supposed to treat you like a massage boy I hired from online, Ko thought. Kitty kept massaging his ass, and Ko managed to keep himself still. It wasn't easy. His cock was hard, and pressed against the table. He tried to recall when that happened, before or after Kitty touched his ass? Whenever it was, he needed to get it in control before the massage was over. It had just been too long since he was with a man. He was always careful on the road, and the past year, his schedule had been packed.

"My legs still hurt a little," he said. "Could you massage them?"

Ko's dick was leaking precum onto the table. He could feel it against his stomach and had no idea how he would hide it from Kitty when he had to move again.

"Is this good?" Kitty asked.

He was at Ko's thighs. Too close.

"Can you do the calves?"

"Sure."

Calves led to feet, where Kitty did something he had never done before. Ko wasn't sure what it was, only that the pressure was having an unusual side effect. He was getting harder. Not just hard, but on the brink of coming. All he needed was a little more pressure.

"That's good," he told Kitty. "You can stop."

"You still look tense."

Kitty's hands returned to Ko's ass. His thumbs alighted along his crack and gently pried it apart. Kitty's tongue flicked Ko's hole, then dove into it. Ko's lower body jerked and sent shock waves through his penis. His animal side overran any thought of telling Kitty to stop, and he didn't make a sound as Kitty sucked his hole open. His tongue felt amazing, better than any cock Ko ever had. Ko clasped the edges of the table and rode Kitty's face to orgasm. He was barely done when Kitty flipped him over and turned him sideways. Kitty had a condom and lube in his pocket, and no underwear on under his pants. His cock was thick, so hard it bobbed under its own weight. He rolled a condom on, and the tip of his cock kissed Ko's hole.

"I cried myself to sleep when I heard you were leaving," He said. "I was like a child. The thought of not seeing you drove me crazy."

"You quit for me?"

"I quit because there was no reason to stay. Tonight was my last chance."

"Then what are you waiting for?" Ko asked. "Make love to me."

The table was low enough, so Ko could wrap his legs around Kitty when he entered. He leaned back a little, and Kitty moved inside him. He wanted to be closer, needed all of Kitty. He told Kitty to bring him to the floor. In an impressive display of strength, Kitty lifted Ko off the table and lowered him without his dick ever leaving Ko's ass. Kitty held Ko against him, hugging him tighter with every stroke until they were both on the edge and begging the other to let go. Ko lost control first, coming between them in heavy spurts.

"Now," he ordered, when he found his voice. "Don't make me wait."

He made Kitty look him in the eyes when he came. It was intense, and Ko found himself coming for a third time, deep in the most private part of himself. He was no longer a kite in the wind. He was in the middle of a storm and being torn apart without mercy. When the clouds cleared, he was limp in Kitty's lap, his hair soaked with sweat. Kitty wasn't even out of breath.

"You haven't kissed me yet," Ko said, needing to say something.

"I kissed you. Just not here."

Kitty kissed him, his lips soft and loving. Ko didn't want to let him go, not then or ever. They could go back to Tokyo together, he thought, that night if they wanted to. Ko would get a job, live openly with Kitty as his boyfriend.

"This is different," he said.

Kitty looked startled. "You've never been with a man before?"

"No! I meant this. We can go home together, wake up together."

"Have you been in hiding so long?"

"Yes."

"Then why don't we go out and celebrate," Kitty said. "Your first night as gay Ko."

"You talk like I'm a virgin," Ko said. "I've been with men. I've had boyfriends. I just didn't talk about it."

"And now?"

"If I have to give up everything I've ever wanted, I want something amazing in return."

The Lunatic Dagon was dead. Long live the Lunatic Dragon. Ko kissed Kitty as a different, equally powerful, need overwhelmed him. He could smell the locker room again, with his and Kitty's personal scent mixed in. It was a better goodbye than he could have ever hoped for.

"Come on," he told Kitty. "Take me home for a private celebration."

SOME LIKE IT ROUGH
By Landon Dixon

Decker stepped off the elevator, saw the two men fighting with each other in the hall; not really fighting, more like slapping. He grinned, advanced on the pair of lovers.

He'd seen them move in a month before, heard them yelling shrilly at each other for the past couple of weeks, even where he lived at the end of the hall. They were both small, blond, tanned, a pair of sweet looking, tight-assed pixies who fought like pumas with one another. Decker could only imagine what their lovemaking was like.

"Hey, what's going on!?" he barked.

The two men turned and stared at him, their blues eyes flashing. They could've been twins — sweet, succulent twins — only one was slightly taller and slimmer, Connor. He seemed to enjoy picking on the other, Billy.

"What business is it of yours!?" Connor flared, planting his small hands on his narrow hips.

Decker cuffed him across the face, knocking the man backwards. "I make it my business, when I have to hear it and see it — you fairies fighting with each other."

Billy's eyes were wide, and his mouth hung open. Connor held a trembling hand up to his cheek.

Decker was a big man, broad-shouldered, wasp-waisted, with dark brown hair and eyes, a ruggedly handsome face complete with a dimpled chin built into a square jaw. He looked tough, capable of handling any trouble, or starting it.

"Hey, you can't ... you can't just ... hit Connor like that!" Billy squealed.

Decker gave him the back of his hand, knocking him against the door of his apartment. "I'll do whatever I want ... to get some peace and quiet around here." He glared at the two blonds. "And don't tell me you pansies didn't like it."

Connor lowered his hand from his face, quivering red lips forming a grin. Billy looked at his lover, at Decker, squirming around like he had to pee — or do something with his cock.

"Let me in," Decker growled. "We're going to settle this right now."

Billy could barely fit the key into the lock. Connor couldn't get into the apartment fast enough.

Decker shoved the pair into the living room, took a look around. The place was done up almost entirely in white — white, overstuffed furniture, thick white carpeting, white walls, a sparkling clean white kitchen leading off from the living room. "Pretty posh," the big man commented, rubbing his dick in his jeans.

"We like it," Connor said. "We've still got some more work to ..."

"Yeah," Decker grunted, cutting him off. He planted his two hands on Connor's rounded shoulders, planted the

86

man down onto his knees in the shag. "I've heard enough out of your mouths. Now I'm going to stick something in."

Billy fell to his knees alongside Connor. The two men started at the massive bulge in Decker's jeans, the expanding outline of his cock. Decker rubbed it, looking down at the men. "Who wants it first?" he said.

Billy's little hands scrambled all over the front of Decker's pants, fumbling the button open, tugging the fly down. The zipper rose up and along the length of Decker's cock, dropping down inches and inches later at his balls. Billy pulled the jeans apart, and Decker's cock flopped out into the open, long and hard and getting longer and harder, swelling up into the air. Billy tried to wrap his hands around it. Decker cuffed him upside the head.

"Don't get greedy, little man. I'll dish out the meat around here."

Both men watched from their knees, as Decker's cock rose higher, engorging, smooth-curved hood bloating and sniffing at the air, smooth-skinned shaft filling up and out, jutting from Decker's loins. Until the man's cock was mammoth full-length, right in front of Billy and Connor's shining faces.

Decker gripped his dick, smacked Connor's face with it.

"Ooh!" Billy murmured.

Decker slapped Billy's face with the huge appendage, the hard-soft impact heating up both men even more. "Stick out your tongues, you pair of cock-sluts!" Decker ordered.

Pink tongues leaped out of red mouths, glistening, trembling, stretching as far as they'd go. Decker smacked the flat of Connor's tongue with his heavy hood, Billy's tongue. "You use your mouths for sucking my dick from now on, not yelling and screaming at one another. Understand?"

The men eagerly nodded, tongues hanging out like a couple of blond puppies.

Decker smacked Connor's right cheek with his wettened dong, whacked Billy's left. "Understand!?"

"Yes! Yes!" the men gulped.

Decker drove his cock into Connor's open mouth, almost right down to the balls. Connor didn't even gag, his mouth and throat like a drain, like Decker had suspected. His lips sealed around shaft, both men thrilling at the feel of cock stuffing mouth.

Decker dug his big hands into his Connor's soft blond hair, his long, powerful fingers clutching tight. Then he pumped his hips, hard, fucking Connor's mouth.

Decker's cock plunged down the blond's hot, wet, tight throat, pulled all the way out to the point of bulbing Connor's straining lips, then plowed all the way back in again. Over and over.

Connor's wide blue eyes went watery. His nostrils flared, gasping for air. His cheeks billowed, throat bulging. Billy watched Decker's cock dive down his lover's throat, engorge his mouth, anxiously holding his own mouth gaping open.

Decker fast-fucked Connor's face, jerking the man's head back and forth, smacking his balls against Connor's chin. Until he abruptly let go of the one blond's head and yanked his cock out, speared it into the other blond's mouth.

Billy took it just as deep, just as delighted. He tried to grab onto Decker's pumping hips, to steady himself. But Decker smacked his hands away, grabbed onto Billy's head and pistoned his face. Drool surged out of the corners of Billy's mouth, the man's plush lips stretched wide, like his mouth and throat to accommodate all that thick, juicy cock.

Connor barely had time to get his breath back, before Decker hit his mouth again, stuffed him full of cock. Decker fucked Connor's mouth, Billy's, plunging deep and pumping hard. The men were dizzy, rocked with sensation. Decker's balls tightened, his gleaming dong coursing cum-hard.

He pulled his dick free and shoved the two men's heads together, stuck his cock in between. So that he was gliding shaft along both sets of lips, both tongues, a man on either side of his thrusting prick.

"Yeah! I'm going to come all over you sluts' faces!" Decker rasped, poling fast and hard in between Connor and Billy, the two men's tongues and lips cushioning, stroking the churning cock. "And you sluts are going to lick each other clean!"

It wasn't a request, it was a command. Connor and Billy urgently bobbed their heads in agreement, never losing mouth contact with Decker's pistoning cock.

Decker grunted, grabbed onto his dick. He twisted Billy's head around, jerked, jetting hot cum into the man's open mouth. He grabbed onto Connor's head, blasted a thick rope of sticky jizz into that man's mouth.

Decker went back and forth, rocked back on his heels by the force of his brutal orgasm, striping Billy's tongue, splattering Connor's nose. The men's faces were coated with cum, their mouths full, and gulping.

They threw their arms around one another and excitedly licked each other off, tonguing simmering cum between them. As Decker dripped the last few drops out of his cock down onto the carpet with a squeeze of his hand, watching with a hard grin on his face.

# # # # #

"Wanna take a ride on my bike?"

Decker turned his head, looked at the man leaning up against the bar. He was huge, leather-clad arms and legs thick with muscle, head a block of granite atop cinder block shoulders, face heavy with beard. He had a red rag tied around the top of his head, a pair of gold nose studs. "Won't your friends mind?" Decker asked, nodding at the table of equally tough-looking bikers ten paces away.

"Fuck 'em," the man grunted, voice guttural as the roar of a Harley. "I ride solo when I wanna. Haul ass with whoever I want."

Decker set his drink down on the chipped counter of the stripper bar. "You aren't too rough, are you?"

The biker grinned gold-plated teeth. He tucked a strand of Decker's soft, brown hair in behind the man's left ear with a sausage-like digit. "Not too rough," he rumbled. "Name's Torrance. Let's get to know each other, huh?"

There was barely room on the back of the chopper for Decker, what with Torrance's massive body filling the leather seat. Decker gripped the sissy bar in behind, as Torrance revved the machine to thunder, released the brake and let the bike leap forward. They roared out of the gravel parking lot and onto the highway, the howl of the engine tearing the night apart.

It was little more than a shack by the edge of the river. Torrance skidded the big bike to a stop on the clay and dumped Decker off the back. Then he kicked out the stand, dismounted, pulled Decker off the ground and pushed him through the slatted door of the shack. "Ain't much, but the road's my home," he said, lighting a kerosene lamp, hanging it on a nail.

Decker glanced around at the sunken cot, the rickety wooden table and pair of chairs and couple of cupboards, the junk strewn all over the dirt floor. "You got that right," he commented.

Torrance strode up from behind, clutched Decker by the back of the head and twisted his face around. He slammed his mouth down onto Decker's open mouth, thrusting his tongue inside and thrashing it around.

Decker had taken all he was going to take. He jarred his palms into Torrance's chest, knocking the bear of a man backwards.

Torrance licked his thick lips, grinning. "You wanna get rough, huh?" He advanced on Decker, raised a paw, swung it.

Decker easily blocked the blow with his arm, landed one of his own, smacking Torrance across the face with the flat of his hand. Torrance's head jerked back, his grey eyes gone wide. Decker smacked him again, and those eyes welled with tears.

"Yeah, I thought so," Decker growled, shoving Torrance back against the wall. The whole shack shook. "Not so tough without a big bike strapped to your crotch. You want it up the ass; you're going to do it my way, pussy."

Torrance wiped his mouth with the back of his hand, staring at Decker. He charged. Decker easily side-stepped, shot out a leg, tripping Torrance, sending the big man sprawling head-first to the ground. Decker strolled over, went down, sinking a knee into the small of Torrance's back, then crashing his hand down onto the biker's wide, mounded ass.

The crack of palm against leather went off like a gunshot. Torrance shuddered, whimpered. Decker whacked Torrance's ass again with the flat of his right hand. The man's broad cheeks rippled beneath the well-worn black leather, the man's body trembling. "Just a big, overgrown baby with his loud toy bike, huh?" Decker gritted.

Torrance shifted, squirmed, but Decker held him pinned down; not that the biker was really trying to escape anyway. Decker hit his ass again, right cheek, then left. Then both at once, whistling his hand down onto Torrance's butt.

He flailed the man's leather-clad ass, turning his hand into a blade that knifed through the air, the hardened palm striking sharply, repeatedly, blazing into the biker's cheeks, shivering the man full of shimmering heat. Torrance jumped with every blow, groaning, thrusting his big bottom up to meet the crushing hand.

"Not hurting you enough, huh?" Decker rasped. "You want it harder, skin-on-skin! You want me to spank your bare ass, don't you, you big, tough biker pussy!?"

He didn't wait for a reply, wedging his burning fingers into the waistband of Torrance's pants and yanking down. As Torrance arched up off the dirt. The leather pants skinned down, butt cheeks popping out into the open, rounded hills trembling with need, pale skin streaked with red where heavy blows had already landed.

"Fuck, hit me!" Torrance groaned, clawing at the dirt.

Decker stared at the man's buttocks, his hand poised, knee back in position on the man's back. "What? Say it louder!"

"Hit me! Fucking spank me!" the sprawled-out biker roared.

Decker grinned, then brought his hand smashing down onto the bare flesh. The shack rattled with the impact, the sound exploding in the men's ears. Torrance jarred into the ground, his butt cheeks rippling violently; never coming to a complete stop, before Decker hit them again, and again, and again.

The big man burst into tears, Decker whacking his ass relentlessly, ruthlessly. Flesh fired crimson, fanned into flame by Decker's hand, filling Torrance with savage pain and pleasure, Decker with raw desire. He wanted to fuck that big ass, stick his hard, throbbing cock between those beaten buttocks and truly pound the man's butt, sear his insides like the outside.

"I'm going to fuck you, Torrance!" he gasped, between blows, sweat pouring off his face.

Torrance could only moan, embroiled in the conflagration consuming his ass and fire-storming through his body. His butt had gone just about numb under the brutal onslaught, each blow hitting him deep inside, striking at the core of who he was, his precarious sexuality. So when Decker's hand didn't bang into his cheeks anymore, it was the worst kind of pain of all.

Decker straddled Torrance's legs, shoved his own pants down to his knees. His cock sprang out into the electrified air, hard as iron. He leaned forward and ripped the biker's doo-rag off, rubbed his hand around in the unwashed, matted hair; greasing his hand, then his cock.

"I'm going to stick my cock in your ass, Torrance — fuck you even harder than I beat you!" he husked, leaning over top of the fallen biker and prodding his shining, swollen hood in between the man's battered cheeks.

Torrance humped his ass upward, meeting Decker's cap with his pucker. Then he pounded the ground with his fists, when Decker pressed down hard. The pressure mounted, the tension soaring to explosive levels, Decker's cockhead squishing against Torrance's starfish. Then bursting through, bulbing ring and sinking into chute. Followed by shaft, inches and inches of bloated cock.

Decker plowed his entire dick into the prone biker, going in slow and sure; not satisfied until his balls kissed up against the man's blistered butt cheeks, then squashed against, his cock fully buried in Torrance's ass. He flattened his palms onto the ground on either side of the wide-body biker and pumped his hips, fucking Torrance's anus.

They both groaned, Decker pumping slow and languorous, bouncing lightly off Torrance's rump. Then torquing up the pace, driving harder and faster, pounding into the biker's gripping, sucking hole.

"You love it up the ass! You love me fucking you up the ass, don't you!?" Decker raged, smashing his body against Torrance's butt.

"Yeah! Fuck, yeah!" the other man cried, pumping his own pulsating appendage into the dirt, in rhythm to the cock sawing his chute.

Decker pistoned faster and faster, now spanking Torrance's buttocks with his thighs almost as viciously as he had with his hand. His cock was a red-hot poker, sticking the biker's anus, going molten inside Torrance's velvet hot tunnel.

"I'm going to come in your ass! I'm going to blast your ass full of my cum!"

"Do it!"

Decker pummeled Torrance, splitting the man in two with his battering-ram cock, reaming chute. Until he jerked, jolted by orgasm, his cock exploding, rupturing white-hot semen into Torrance's anus.

The biker felt the scalding spurts, and he grunted, shuddering with his own orgasm, his own cock going off and spraying into the ground.

The two men emptied out their balls, Decker filling Torrance's beaten-down ass, Torrance pouring out his pent-up lust into the dirt.

# # # # #

Decker spotted the kid slouched against the side of a building, barely visible on the edges of the halo of light shed by a sagging street lamp. It was night, rain pouring down, the area the urban shithole. Decker's cock was hard and hungry in his pants as he slowly cruised by.

He went down an alley and came out onto the street opposite, drove back around. This time, he slowed to a stop at the crumbling curb, alongside the kid. He thumbed down the window and yelled, "Hey, you need a ride or anything!?"

The kid looked up from beneath his wide-brimmed cap. His face was young, pretty, dark as the night itself, eyes wide and showing white, lips plush and wet with a nervous lick from a neon-pink tongue. "Huh?" He looked like a runaway.

Decker shifted the car into park, turned off the engine, got out. He'd liked the look of that empty alley for what he had in mind. The street shone slick with rain, some whores up at the corner, but no one else around. The kid was wearing a baggy basketball tank top and shorts, sneakers. The smooth, ebony skin on his arms and legs gleamed with moisture.

"What's your name?" Decker asked, walking up.

"Fuck business is it of yours!?"

Decker slapped the kid's cap off his head, revealing a burr of black hair. He looked eighteen, maybe nineteen. "Don't mouth off to me, punk!"

"Anthony. My name's Anthony. So what?"

"So this," Decker rasped, grabbing the kid by a bare arm and dragging him down the sidewalk to the mouth of the alley, shoving him in. His cock was a pulsing pole in his jeans, driving him on.

Anthony stared at Decker, his lean body shaking. He bathed his lips with that pink tongue again. Decker shoved him up against the greasy wall of the alley, mashed his mouth into the kid's mouth.

"Hey! What the fuck!?" Anthony squealed, trying to wriggle away.

"Don't tell me you aren't selling it!" Decker hissed, pinning the kid's shoulders against the grimy wall. He kissed him again, hard, shoving his tongue inside the young man's mouth and tasting hot spit.

"Okay! Okay!" Anthony gasped, gulping humid air when Decker at last broke mouth contact. "What you want, man?"

Decker grinned into the kid's frightened-looking face. "I want it all. Only I'm not paying a cent for it." He pressed down on Anthony's bony shoulders, pushing him down to the cobblestones. He pulled his erection out, smacked Anthony's face with it, stuffed it into Anthony's open mouth.

"Suck it, baby! Suck it!" he growled, the delicious heat and wetness enveloping his dong and suffusing his body. He gripped Anthony's ears and moved the kid's head back and forth, moving his own hips, fucking face.

Until he suddenly felt a sharp pain in his cock. His eyes burst open, and he stared down, astonished. The kid was biting into his dick, shaft half in and half out of Anthony's mouth, sharp white teeth sunk right into the middle. "Hey, what the ..."

"Fuck!" Decker screamed, the kid biting his cock almost in two.

Anthony's lips curled up at the corners, into a grin, his teeth embedded in Decker's dong. Now, he moved his head back and forth on his own, scraping his teeth along Decker's shaft.

Decker went rigid, unable to do anything for fear of getting his cock bitten right off, at the mercy of the young man.

Anthony pulled his head all the way back, finally releasing Decker's cock. But before the older man could regain control of the situation, Anthony grabbed onto his balls and roughly twisted them. He rose to his feet, bringing Decker up onto the toes of his feet. Then he spun the man around and shoved him up against the wall.

"I'm a cop, tough guy!" he hissed in Decker's ear. He pulled the man's arms back, slapped handcuffs onto his wrists before Decker could react. "I should take you in, book you for soliciting, and assault!"

Decker froze against the wall.

Anthony grinned. "Lucky for you, I'm a dirty cop. You like it rough, huh? Well, sucker, you're going to get it rough."

Anthony popped Decker's jeans fully open, plunged them down the man's legs, exposing Decker's ass.

"Hey, no … this isn't the way it's supposed to go down!" Decker whined.

"Not your way, man. My way."

Decker heard a metallic click, then felt something cool probe in between his quivering butt cheeks. Anthony had snapped out his retractable baton, was pushing the tip of it into Decker's pale buttocks, pressing the tip up against the man's asshole.

Decker crumbled like a schoolyard bully. "Stick it in! Fuck me!" he pleaded, his bluff called; but being on the receiving end just as ripe with possibilities as the other way around.

Anthony pushed the knob of the baton through Decker's pucker, into the man's ass. Decker cried out, the cold metal shocking his hot anus. Anthony pumped back and forth, fucking Decker's chute with the baton, not too deep, but deep enough.

"Stick it all the way in!" Decker begged.

Anthony pulled the baton out, slammed Decker up against the wall. "I'm in charge here, asshole! And the only thing going to go all the way up your tight, white ass is my big, black dick! You want that, right?!"

Decker nodded, his anus burning empty.

Anthony took a quick look around. The alley was empty, like the street beyond, the shadows deep. He pushed his basketball shorts down. His cock hung long, thick, engorged. He pulled a tube of lube out of a pocket and oiled the snake, letting Decker twist his head around to get a good look.

Anthony's cock stiffened up huge in his stroking hand. "I'm going to stick every last inch into your ass, white boy. And you're going to like it."

Decker whimpered, turning his face back to the wall. He'd been giving it out, now he was going to get it back, big-time. He jumped when he felt Anthony's slippery fingers slide up against his crack, groaned with pleasure when he felt two of those fingers plunge right into his ass.

"Better get you loosened up some, huh?" Anthony breathed in Decker's ear, pressing the pair of digits three knuckles deep into Decker's tight, pink anus. Then he pumped, finger-fucking the man.

Decker moaned into the brick, his body electrified. Anthony plowed his fingers in and out of Decker's chute. He pumped him hard, ramming him up against the wall, ramming his ass.

Decker wallowed in it, rode it, his own cock hard as the wall in front of him. He loved getting churned, his ass blazing with sensation.

Anthony yanked his fingers free and grabbed up his dong, slammed the mushroomed tip into Decker's pucker. His fingers had done the work; his shiny blue-black cap stretched Decker's starfish still more and then was immersed in anus. "Here it comes, motherfucker!"

"Stick your cock up my ass!"

Anthony gritted his teeth and drove his prick into Decker's ass, gleaming licorice stick gliding inside, more and more and more. Decker felt like his insides were being torn apart, all that cock filling his chute. Anthony felt the wicked gripping pressure, the resistance, but kept on pushing forward. Until all that showed on the end of Decker's white ass were Anthony's big black balls.

Anthony grated, "Now you're getting what you deserve," moving his hips back, pushing them forward, pile-driving Decker's ass.

Decker moaned and writhed, so wanting to grab onto his own vibrating cock and stroke, but prohibited from doing so. His ass felt as if it'd been pumped full to twice its normal size, wonderful sensations rippling up from his stuffed anus and flooding his body and brain.

Anthony gripped Decker's shoulders, shunted his massive cock in the man's chute. He bit his lip, moving faster, fucking harder, his face a glistening mask of sexual concentration.

The men grunted and groaned, Decker's buttocks shivering with the impact of Anthony's thighs striking against them, his body shivering with the impact of all that cock fucking his butt. He cried, spasmed, his own cock suddenly going off, hands-free, blistering-raw orgasm blazing through his body on the tip of that wildly thrusting dong.

Anthony grinned madly, slamming Decker's quivering ass, fucking in a frenzy. His flapping balls tingled, erupted. Pure, white-hot ecstasy shot out the end of his pumping cock, dousing him in erotic emotion, as he doused Decker's bowels.

# # # # #

Decker had learned to take it; take it and love it. Just so long as it was rough.

TO THE RESCUE
By Landon Dixon

Briscoe shoved me up against the tree, growled, "You're gonna take it and like it, punk!"

I grabbed the smooth birch bark behind me, pleading, "No, please! I-I don't want any part of this!"

I was dressed in a white T-shirt and cuffed blue jeans, my short brown hair neatly parted down the middle, sun browned body neatly packaged in the innocent get-up. Briscoe was decked out in a faded and torn leather jacket, greasy black jeans, his big bald head shining menacingly under the park light pole, his goatee snapped to a point with an elastic band, wide body stretching the jacket and pants.

We were just off the beaten path, to the side of a park bench, Briscoe pinning me to the tree with the force of his body and words. He slapped my face.

"You're a part of it, punk!" he sneered. "And you're gonna put out — or I'm gonna put you out!"

I tried to squirm away from him, but his huge left hand gripped my tee at the neck, clutching cotton and skin. He thrust his belligerent head forward and smashed his thick, wet lips into my lips.

I twisted my head to the side, and his hungry mouth found my cheek, my ear, his tongue swarming inside, rattling me right down to my sneakers. "No! Please! This wasn't … what I had in mind!"

His breath steamed in my ear, "Wasn't what you had in mind!? You parade around outside a biker bar, shaking that cute little skintight ass of yours, and you don't expect no one to take the bait? Don't fuckin' make me laugh, punk!"

His tongue washed all over my cheek, then forced its way between my lips again, from the side. He mashed his hot, hard body against mine, and I could feel the rigid length of his cock in his jeans, pressing, pumping into my groin.

"Please! Get off me! I'll yell, I'll scream!"

"I like 'em yellin' and screamin'. Gets me all excited." Briscoe whipped my head around to face him again, slammed his mouth into mine. He pumped me hard against the tree, cock driving into my cock.

A shadow moved far away down the otherwise empty park path, coming closer, moving faster.

Briscoe jerked his head back to suck some air into his lungs, and I bleated, "I think someone's coming! You'd better … you'd better stop!"

He roughly tongued my trembling lips with his sticker, used his own swollen lips to snarl, "The only one comin' is gonna be me."

He ripped my T-shirt up out of my jeans, locked his heavy hands onto my smooth-shaven pecs, mauled them, slashing his tongue across one puffy nipple, the other one. I writhed against the tree, watching through slitted eyes that shadow down the path grow larger, form into a man as it passed under a park light − a tall, well-built man, running now, towards us.

Briscoe tore at my nipples with his lips and teeth. Then, he released my mounded pecs and grabbed onto my shoulders, shoving me down to my knees in the grass. "You're gonna blow me, punk!" he grated. "Or I'm gonna blow you away. Understand?"

He pulled his pants open and yanked his hard cock out into the open. He slapped my face with the turgid slab of beef, smacked my head back the other way. I opened my mouth to warn him about the man again — only fifty feet away and closing at a gallop — and Briscoe rammed his dong inside of me, driving down the back of my throat.

I didn't choke, didn't gag, didn't give him that pleasure. His hairy balls slapped up against my chin, his throbbing meat bulging my cheeks and engorging my throat. My wide blue eyes peeled to the side, staring at the rushing man only fifteen feet away now.

He was well over six-feet tall, broad-shouldered and narrow-waisted. He had short, glossy black hair that shone in the yellow park light, a smooth, handsome face dimpled at the chin, dark eyes that glittered. He was wearing a light grey jacket and a dark-blue shirt and a black pair of pants. His clothing fit his impressive physique like a custom-made glove.

Briscoe grabbed my ears and churned his hips back and forth, brutally reaming my mouth and throat. "Now that's more fuckin' like ..."

A manicured hand clamped down on his shoulder, spun him around. Briscoe's cock flew out of my gasping mouth. "It takes two willing partners to tango," my new hero intoned. "And, in case you hadn't noticed, this is a public park. Hardly the place for what you had in mind."

Briscoe gaped at the guy, his cock dangling slick with my saliva, all the evidence the intervening man needed. "Hey, asshole, why don't you ..."

The man's right hand was a blur as it shot into Briscoe's stomach. Briscoe bent double, spewing hot air. The man brought his left fist up in a crushing uppercut before I could even say anything, catching Briscoe on the point of his goatee and sending him sailing, slamming down onto his back; out cold.

"Hey, we were just playacting!" I tried to explain, bouncing my astonished eyes between my unconscious lover and the new man in my life. The new man won, his good looks and body just too much to ignore. "Role ... playing," I mumbled. "He wasn't actually hurting me."

"Dirk Mantle's the name," tall, dark, and wickedly handsome proclaimed, extending a welcoming hand, his lush, red lips revealing a charming smile. "No need to thank me. Any citizen would have done the same."

"But-but ..." I took one last look at my laid-out lover. He was snoring comfortably. So I reached out and gripped Dirk's hand, was enveloped in dry, confident heat, as he pumped my arm.

He released my hand, and winked, turned and started walking away. I stared at his tight, clenching butt cheeks, the light illuminating them on their way.

Okay, if he wouldn't buy the truth, then I'd play up the lie. I just had to get to know this man better. The yearning impulse in my pants made that an imperative. I dashed after him.

"I-I want to thank you for what you did!" I pleaded, barely catching up with his long, powerful stride. "I mean, really thank you."

He shook his head. "No need. Just doing my duty — as a citizen of this city and connoisseur of this park."

I licked my wooden lips and swallowed dry, struggling to keep pace with the gorgeous, glorious man. I grabbed onto his hand again, thrilling at the touch of his warm, smooth skin. "I mean, I'm willing to do anything — to thank you."

He squeezed my hand and broke away, striding faster, gaining ground away from desperate me.

"Oral, anal … you name it!" I blurted, frantic to stop him in his tracks, get him moving in rhythm to me. "I'll suck your cock and then you can butt-fuck me any way you want!"

It didn't phase him in the least. My open-ended invitation was left crumpled on the city park path, as Dirk Mantle steamed relentlessly onward, leaving me despairing in his manly wake.

# # # # #

I was back in the park the following evening, with a different dance partner this time.

"You're not really going to hit me or anything, are you?" Leonard whined.

The sawed-off nerd with the horn-rimmed glasses was a friend of mine. He was getting paid for his performance — a free dinner — but he wasn't the best actor for this type of business. But he was all I had. "No, no, don't worry about it," I rasped, looking up and down the park path, not seeing anyone.

The location was the same, by the birch tree next to the bench, the hour identical to the night before. But there wasn't a soul in sight, least of all Dirk Mantle and his starring face and body.

I figured maybe the bait had to be flopping around a bit, to attract the hero to the scene. So I slapped Leonard across the face.

"Ouch!" he wailed, even though I'd only tiffed him.

"Remember the pasta at Angelo's you're going to be stuffing down your face!" I hissed, slapping his other cheek with my fingertips. Snapping my glance back and forth between the two ends of the footpath.

Leonard petulantly pushed me back. "They don't even have a buffet there anymore."

"Huh?" I smacked him a good one across the chops, glancing left, right.

He jolted me backwards with his two hands.

"Hey, what are you doing!? You're not supposed to fight back."

"Then quit hitting me!"

I stared at the guy. "I'm going to do worse than that, you stupid punk! Angelo's doesn't come cheap!" I thumped him up against the tree trunk, backhanded his glasses to the very end of his pointy nose.

He fought back, pounding his little fists into my chest.

I grabbed onto his Batman tee at the neck and rattled his head back, smacking his hands aside. "Listen, you little ..."

"I really hate to see a bigger man pick on a smaller one," someone stated right behind us. In a clear, clarion voice of righteous indignation.

I spun around, stared at Dirk. I'd completely forgotten about the man in my spat with Leonard.

Now I remembered what it was all about, Dirk's muscled body in a green polo shirt and tan pair of pants filling my eyes, my pants. "Why don't you mind your own business, asswipe!" I growled. The words were hard to say, but they had to be said. If I couldn't entice the man by playing nice, then I'd play bad.

"Can I go now?" Leonard wheezed, fumbling for his Rotahaler.

I was about to say, Yeah, get the heck out of here. But I thought better of it. "You'll go when I say you can go, punk!"

I grabbed onto Dirk's chest, filling my hands with the fine-woven cloth of his shirt, the fine-chiseled humps of his pecs. "And just what the hell do you think you're going to do about it?" I asked him.

109

He flipped me around, into a stranglehold, using some sort of Oriental technique probably taught to him at the Buddhist monastery he'd been raised in some rocky and remote part of Tibet. His body pressed tightly against mine from behind, his bare arms entwining my neck and chest. I was in heaven, the grasp of a god.

"Yes, you can go now, sir," he told Leonard, his rich voice filling my red, beating ear, vibrating all through my inflamed body. "He won't bother you anymore."

Leonard pocketed his Rotahaler and straightened his glasses. "Remember about Ang ..."

"Get out of here!" I hissed.

Dirk tightened his grip. Risking snappage of the spine, I undulated my butt against the man, bumping my twin taut mounds into his groin. Thrilling when my sensitive cheeks detected some actual growth there.

Dirk must have felt it, too, because he spun me back around, held me at arm's length. "I trust you've learnt your lesson?"

I wanted to learn more, so much more. "You ain't taught me nuthin' yet, asshole!" I spat.

I slammed my hands up into Dirk's arms, popping his grip loose. Then I ducked my head down and tackled the guy. We landed on the soft bed of grass with a whoomp, me on top of my hero.

His hard, hot body beat underneath me, and I pressed my temporary advantage home, pumping my pumped-up cock against his loins, against his cock. He had swelled up considerably, already my length only semi-erect. I just about swooned in the man's arms, hugging him close, shunting my pulsating dong along his cock in his tight pants.

He quickly regained his leverage and rolled over on top of me. My advantage still, even better. His big body covered my heaving form completely, pinning me deliciously to the earth. I thrust upwards, dropping my hands down onto his rugged buttocks and gripping the hard-mounded pair and squeezing for all I was worth, using that leverage to fast-pump my prick into his prick.

He breathed hotly in my face, his beautiful visage only inches above. He was hesitating, unsure what was happening, but now sure as I was to his definite arousal. His cock was enormous in his pants, and I slid my own dick up and down its awesome length.

I bobbed my head up and kissed the man on the mouth. His lips were plush and moist and lovely, a place to park a man's mouth forever. Dirk bladed a hand under my chin and choked me off in mid-smooch.

He had me pinned at an awkward angle. New tactics were called for. I fluttered my eyelids shut and went suddenly limp beneath the super-man. Then started convulsing, gasping for air.

It worked! He released the numbing pressure on my neck and replaced it with lip pressure on my mouth. He breathed in and out into me, performing mouth-to-mouth resuscitation. My cock ballooned with lust against his, his luscious breath filling my body, his lovely lips sealing tight and delightful.

I shuddered, like I was still fighting for my life. When really it was just a good old-fashioned man-on-man sex shudder, my body ablaze with the wonderful sensations of my hero kissing me, breathing into me, pressing against me with his cock, his body draped all over me.

Dirk pulled his head back, giving me a chance to breathe on my own. I lolled my tongue out of the side of my mouth and convulsively clutched his buttocks, spasming my cock against his. My eyes popped open, rolled back in my head.

Dirk pressed his mouth back over mine again, his lips squeezing down onto my tongue. He huffed and puffed. I chuffed cock-to-cock, clenching tight to his rump.

I surged with tingling heat, dick gone cum-hard against Dirk's hard dick. It wasn't the prettiest of lovemaking — one man faking his own death while he felt up and frotted another trying to save him. But it was getting the job done, big-time.

I moaned into Dirk's mouth, bucking beneath him. I was past the point of no return. I didn't see a white light, though, I saw stars, in the sky and in mind. Exploding, as my furiously rubbing prick went off against Dirk's steely length, and I blasted sweet ecstasy into my pants and against his cock.

I jerked repeatedly with joy, his mouth consuming my mouth, his body enveloping my body. While everything else had been faked that glorious night, there was no faking the wicked orgasm I was experiencing. I came so hard and so heavy I almost did pass out, for real.

Dirk pulled me to my feet afterwards, and I staggered up against my hero. "I hope you've learned your lesson now," he stated resolutely.

"Teach me more!" I gasped. "Please, teach me more!"

He steadied me straight and then strode away.

But just before he disappeared into the warm embrace of the night and the misty recesses of my sexual memory, he turned and said, "I'm moving to a different apartment tomorrow. So I won't be taking my strolls in this park anymore. So behave yourself — okay?"

He winked, and he was gone.

180 AD
By Rob Rosen

Rob Rosen (www.therobrosen.com), award-winning author of six novels and editor of two anthologies, has had short stories featured in more than 180 anthologies.

Six buried in my family alone. No neighbors to my immediate east remained, only a handful to the west. A pox of some sort, fever hot as Etna's lava, death all too slow to rear its vile head once the disease took hold. Still, we did our best to keep them comfortable until Pluto took their souls. Which was why I was at the spring that day, wetting strips of cloth to keep my cousin's head cool. And it was then I spotted him, her as well. He was high above, she in the fields beneath.

"Is she not beautiful, friend?" the stranger asked as I approached.

I stared down, squinting into the broiling midday sun. In truth, she was homely, squat and hunched, her clothes frayed. "I think Apollo is playing tricks on you, friend," I replied, praying it wasn't the pox eating away at his mind. Then again, he looked hale enough. And then some, in fact.

He gazed from me to her and back again, and then grinned, his smile as bright as that seething overhead sun. "I fear Apollo has abandoned us, friend," he said. "He and his brethren, I believe. Left us to this plague of Antonine."

That is what the disease had become to be known as, brought back by our troops while on campaign out east it appeared. Already the emperor had succumbed. I nodded my head and frowned. "I hear that two thousand a day are dying in Rome, the army decimated." And it was then that I understood why he said what he had said. I pointed down to the field below. "She is more healthy than beautiful, yes?"

He sighed and shrugged, his wide expanse of shoulders rising and falling. "We must repopulate, yes? Before the land is left empty, before our enemies outnumber us."

In truth, I hadn't given it much thought. Though what he said was most certainly true. And suddenly, my bachelorhood seemed selfish, an affectation reserved for much better times than these. So, I stared from him to her, though he was surely more pleasant to gaze upon and noticed nothing glinting on her marriage finger. "I suppose she has a beauty about her, friend."

He chuckled, the sound rumbling through me like thunder from a storm. His hand was then held out in greeting. "Agapius," he informed. "And at least she is solidly built."

Not the finest compliment but still. I gripped his hand and returned the smile in kind. "Julianus," said I. "Pray she is not barren then, or else her compliments will wilt as sure as the grapes she is picking."

His hand remained in mine, though the smile diminished by half. "I suppose I should go woo this, um, lass then."

And my smile grew weaker as well. "Or perhaps it should be I."

And then both smiles vanished altogether. "Except that it was I who saw her first."

"And I second," I replied. "What of it? It is only who meets her next that matters."

Oddly, his hand remained in mine, a tension behind it that seemed to outweigh the impasse we'd stumbled across. In any case, his smile did make a triumphant reappearance, my own quick to follow, cock stirring in its wake. "So who shall it be then, Julianus? You or I? We are of the same age, from the same stock, apparently, so both would make capable fathers."

"And we're both still alive, praise Jupiter," I added, at last releasing my hand from his, the tension, however, still palpable.

"Praise Jupiter, yes," he agreed. "So what shall determine the outcome of our dilemma then? A game of chance? A test of strength? A gladiatorial battle?"

Again I stared her way, her basket filling of grapes, sweat soaking her back and forehead, hunch even more pronounced now. I grimaced and replied, "Well, certainly nothing to the death, friend. Not for the likes of her."

He laughed and patted my back, face so close I could see the sparkle in his azure eyes, smell the cloves on his sweet breath. "Yes, something less, shall we say, fatal would be in order." He paused and appeared lost in thought, then snapped his fingers and again patted my back. "A wrestling match, Julianus. Still gladiatorial, though without the need for spears or horses."

"Good thing," chided I. "What with my vast array of spears left at home and all." I laughed then considered his offer. "Still, apart from witnessing the occasional wrestling match in the arena, I know little of the sport."

"What is there to know?" he asked. "We grapple and you try to pin me, flatten my shoulders to the ground. We are of equal size and strength, I'd imagine. Should be a fair test in order to win the lady yonder." He pointed to the lady in question, though neglected to look her way. I think we'd both had our full of her beauty for the time being. There'd be plenty of time during the mating for that, I reasoned. All too plenty, in fact.

I nodded at his reasoning, which did in fact appear sound. Then a new thought hit me, just as a gulp slid down my arid throat. "The gladiators wrestle in the nude, Agapius. And oiled up, if I'm not mistaken."

The smile grew even wider upon his impossibly handsome face, like the Greek's Adonis on a really good day. He then reached down to his satchel. "I've just come from town, Julianus," he proclaimed, reaching inside to retrieve a stoppered bottle. "Olive oil, to rub on my horse's flanks." A flush of red spread up his neck. "Or yours."

My gulp repeated. Still, a competition of some sort was needed, so why not this one? It was as good as any, I thought. And right near a spring, to quench our thirst afterward, to wash the oil off. It was as if the Fates were decreeing it. I held my hand out to him yet again. "A wrestling match it is, Agapius. And may the best man, and soon to be father, win."

He took my hand and shook it heartily. "Good luck to you then, Julianus."

All things considered, I'd sorely need it. Either way you looked at it.

So, he backed up, and I backed up, until there was ten feet of flat earth and sparse grass between us. He kicked off his leather sandals, as did I, and then set about to unstring his tunic, an ample swathe of curly hair revealed, then a chest like boulders, a cleft running down the center, a flat belly etched with muscle soon thereafter, before the material was set to the ground behind him. I aped the maneuver, chest rapidly rising and falling as our eyes stayed locked.

Now shirtless, he reached for his leather trousers, the ties released, the material pushed down and off, also kicked behind him as his hooded cock and hanging balls swayed back and forth. Once again, I followed suit, until both of us were naked, grass tickling my bare feet as the sun beat down on us, illuminating the impending spectacle.

Again he bent down, this time to pick up the bottle of olive oil. He unstopped it and poured some of the contents in his hands, said hands then administering the oil far and yon, dead center last, all while I watched and waited my turn. He looked up and caught my eye, fingers still on his dangling prick. "Smooth," he coughed out.

"Shame your horse will go without though," I retorted, with a nervous chuckle quick to follow.

"Though you will surely not," he replied, again closing the gap between us, the bottle handed over.

I took it from him, trying my best not to stare at all that glistening exposed flesh. How do the gladiators make it through the day? I wondered to myself. "Thank you," I said instead, rubbing the oil in. It was, as he said, smooth. And, suffice to say, quite aromatic. Also necessary, I was soon to discover, so that the earth barely nicked you as you squirmed about atop it. Rocks and pebbles slid away as opposed to jabbing on through. I guessed the gladiators were smarter than they looked. Or just enjoyed being oiled up like a precooked sow. Probably the latter, I figured.

I momentarily stared down into the field. Our lady was still picking joylessly away. Then I looked at him, his body fairly radiating, muscles even more defined beneath the layer of pressed olive juice. Distracting, to say the least. "Ready?" he asked.

I shrugged and took a wide stance, arms out, hands open. "As I'll ever be." Which was to say, not at all. Still, it would've been sad for all those olives to have died in vain. I sped ahead, hoping to take him off guard, except he'd done exactly the same thing, and we ended up more like two bulls charging, bodies colliding as we both exhaled sharply and locked horns, as it were. His hands were behind my neck, mine behind his, asses jutting out, both of us staring dead ahead. With his eyes so mesmerizingly blue, it was no wonder that I quickly lost my concentration, and he was able to slip out of my grip and drop me down to the ground.

"Oomph!" I managed, wind knocked out of me as I found myself beneath him, flailing as I attempted to keep my shoulders above the ground and to ignore the fact that his entire body was now pressed up tight to my own, cocks grinding together.

In other words, when I did finally manage to throw him off me, both of us suddenly on our backs, it was readily apparent that our cocks were now rigid as tree limbs, his squatter and fatter than my own, mine longer, both dehooded and slick with olive oil.

"It must be excited at the prospect of copulating with the grape picker," he explained, huffing and puffing as he lay there, staring from his erection to my own.

"Yes, that must be it," I agreed, spotting my chance for an easy pin. Up I hopped, and over, landing on top of him as I fought to place his hands above his head, all while sitting on his chest, rigid prick slapping at his chin. "She's mine!" I shouted.

"And she'd be lucky to have you, apparently," he said, eyeing the beast. "Except that she's mine!" And with that, he raised his feet, locked them with my chest, and pushed me backwards.

Only, when he went to pounce, I rolled away just in the nick of time. He landed flat on the ground, I landed on his back, my cock grinding into his hairy ass, my chin on his neck as I fought to catch my breath. "Wrong side," I managed.

He chuckled and strained to get on all fours in an attempt to once again flip me off of him. With a mighty heave, I flipped, he flipped, and two bodies went tumbling and crashing. When the dust had settled, somehow I still managed to have the advantage. In a manner of speaking that is. For while I was again on my back and he on his front, our torsos were now feet apart and my cock was no longer at his chin, but somehow reversed.

"You smell of lunch, my friend," I chided.

"And as to taste?" he asked, turning his head to the side.

"Hmm," I hummed, popping his thick prick inside my mouth before he pushed it down my throat, the flesh pulsing within, throbbing as I yanked on his heavy balls. When I at last came up for air, I added, "A meatier lunch than I am accustomed to but no less satisfying."

He nodded and gave a chuckle. "A compliment to the chef, to be certain, but now time to end this match of ours, I would think." And then he leapt, suddenly landing on his knees at my side, my right leg instantly lifted up, my knee at my chest as he pushed down hard, his free hand aiming for my left shoulder in attempt to force my torso flat with the ground.

Except I wasn't done in so quickly, and I turned to the side, my right shoulder up in the air. It hurt, yes, but it prevented the pin, though it didn't prevent him from moving from my side to the exposed area between my legs. With one leg up and one down, the entirety of my privates were now exposed.

His hand grasped my swollen prick as my breath sucked in, eyelids fluttering in response. When I again opened them, I found that his face was moving closer and closer to my own, until his impossibly full lips were pressed flush with mine. Oh, could a mere mortal experience such divinity? Had Cupid himself shot his arrow through my chest?

A series of deftly applied strokes were quick to follow, and with a final one, my cock shot, a stream of white-hot sap spewing up before landing on my oil covered chest and belly.

He shot as well as he grinded against the area between cock and balls, moaning loudly in my mouth, exhaling down my lungs as his semen dripped over my side to the ground below, both of us locked so tightly together it was impossible to tell where he ended and I began.

He opened his eyes and moved his head an inch in reverse, the smile beguiling. "Pin, Julianus."

I moved my face from side to side, my shoulders flat on the ground now. "Pluto be damned," I cursed. "It would seem I was distracted."

"A consolation prize, we will call it," he said, stroking my cheek before hopping up. "But now, on to my winnings."

He did not smile as he washed in the spring, as he dressed, his eyes still locked with mine. Then, with his sandals at last on his feet, he helped me to my own. "May your children someday rule the land, Agapius," said I, both of us staring down to the field below, the lady's basket now full.

He turned from her to me and winked. "Perhaps she has a sister that has survived the pox," he said, patting my bare and dusty back.

I sighed and again stared her way. "Perhaps." And then I grinned and pointed, a second women appearing from the edge of the field, looking much like the first. "And perhaps Apollo hasn't abandoned us after all."

We both stood there and watched as the second woman ran to the first, the first waving and smiling, her basket set to the ground. Then, the second was hugging the first tightly, and then kissing her, deeply, and not at all sisterly, much to our surprise.

"Huh," sighed Agapius.

"Seems that the Gods were having their way with us today, friend," said I.

He turned and wrapped his arms around me. "Or the Fates," he purred, his lips again brushing mine, our tongues intertwined in moments.

"And aren't wrestling matches the best two out of three?" I asked, when we'd broken free, if only by a hair.

"You're on," he replied, already kicking off his sandals and untying his tunic. "And may the Gods smile on you this time, Julianus."

I smiled widely, knowing full well that they already had.

WHOPPED
By Jay Starre

Residing on English Bay in Vancouver, Canada, Jay Starre has pumped out steamy gay fiction for dozens of anthologies and has written two gay erotic novels. Contact: Jay Starre on Facebook.

The Fight

"I don't intend on beating that arrogant Argentinian by decision. I'm planning on doing much more. I am going to drag his butt down to the mat, and I am going to submit him. I am going to destroy him. He is going to beg for mercy. He is going to get whopped."

Dean "Submission" Reynolds wasn't merely blustering for the cameras. He had a brutal submission record — and rarely won by decision. To the contrary, his opponent, Raul Montenegro, was renowned for his ability to rack up the points through strikes. His wins were almost always by decision. He'd been victorious by submission only twice in his entire career.

Dean's boast was repeated on the sports channels relentlessly during the week leading up to their bout. The upcoming fight quickly became known as the "whopped" battle. Raul was the welterweight champion and Dean merely an upstart contender, but his challenge had set the combat sports world on fire. Staged in Montreal where the Canadians were ferocious fans of mixed martial arts, the show would be spectacular.

The octagon was lit up with blue as the pair of fighters entered. Music blared as each paraded in, prancing and dancing to the music. The crowd cheered wildly for the main event, both of the fighters claiming their own loyal adherents. Wearing their sweats, they entered the octagon amidst the tumult. It was time to strip.

The younger contender removed his outer clothing first. Dean was a green-eyed red-head with luminescent white skin. Solid muscle, he'd chosen to wear a skimpy pair of snug ruby red shorts that were practically a second skin. The crowd howled when he revealed them, everyone aware that the skimpy trunks were a clear taunt at his opponent who was renowned for wearing outlandish and equally skin-tight shorts. Grinning broadly, the red-head was pleased he'd apparently stolen Raul's thunder, although it was in an admittedly minor way.

Raul grinned back as he stripped down in his corner of the octagon. He even winked as he revealed his own awesome body, longer and leaner with a smooth honey-brown glow that contrasted nicely with the electric blue shorts he sported. Snugly clinging to his muscular ass, they were as expected, but even skimpier than usual and adorned with lightning strikes of bright gold.

It was time for the fight to begin. The announcer offered his usual extended and dramatic call out while the crowd ogled the nearly naked combatants and sized up their chances.

"Introducing first, fighting out of the blue corner, this man is a Tae Kwon Do and mixed martial artist with a professional record of thirty-seven wins and three losses. Fighting out of New York City, he stands six-feet-one-inches and weighing in at one-hundred-sixty-nine pounds, we have the current welterweight champion Raul "Striker" Montenegro!"

When the crowd's shrieks died down, he continued.

"And in the red corner, this man is a college wrestling champion and Jiu-jitsu expert with a professional record of twelve wins and two losses. Fighting out of Baton Rouge, Louisiana, he stands five-feet-elven-inches tall and weighing in at one-hundred-seventy-two pounds, we have Dean "Whop Him" Reynolds!"

Dean smirked as the crowd took in the nickname change his manager had approved at the last minute. His "whopped" remark would not be forgotten, especially if he was victorious tonight!

In the final few moments while the referee was introduced before the battle would begin, Dean performed his usual mental ritual, something most fighters practiced – although his routine was perhaps unique.

He faced Raul and smiled wickedly as he mentally imagined reaching out and tearing off the fighter's electric-blue shorts to reveal his cock and balls and ass. He imagined forcing the fighter to the mat, rolling him over onto his belly, kicking his thighs apart, pulling out his stiff cock and driving it deep into the grinning Argentinian's ass. He would then fuck him relentlessly, slamming his cock home, until Raul would tap out his submission as he shot a creamy load all over the mat.

Of course, Raul had no idea what Dean was thinking.

The fight began. They came out swinging, with both men dancing around the octagon in a display of athletic vigor that quickly became a brawl as their differing strategies collided. Raul had longer arms and legs and was a great volume striker with his six inch reach advantage. Dean was shorter and more solid with his tenacious strength giving him a decided advantage in the wrestling department. Moreover, Dean was rash and young compared to the cool-headed and older champion.

The two combatants were both undeniably good looking in their respective ways. Dean's short hair emphasized his wide-set green eyes and long nose. A small patch of red hair down the center of his chin set off his lush mouth. Raul's thick auburn hair framed a broad face with dark eyes and brilliant white teeth. One was pale and stocky while the other was golden and lean. Both were quickly drenched in sweat, which glistened under the brilliant lights.

The first two rounds went much as anticipated. Even so, it was an exciting battle that had the crowd shrieking. Much of the time it seemed as if it was going all Raul's way, with constant strikes landing on the younger red-head, both from fists and feet. But, Dean did manage a few of his own, especially when Raul moved in too closely. The first round belonged completely to Raul. Yet the young fighter proved himself a real warrior —fighting back even though he was taking a beating with Raul landing so many significant strikes.

During the second round, the young challenger completed two big take-downs that had the crowd on their feet.

The third and final round began with Raul well ahead, and Dean in a precarious position. It would be nearly impossible for him to win by decision at this point. But, the young fighter had never intended on winning by decision. It had always been his goal to submit his opponent.

There were a number of reasons why Dean preferred to win by submission. Technically, it was his best strategy with his shorter limbs, stockier body and incredible physical strength. Psychologically, he felt empowered by the finality of it, the thrill of completely overpowering a strong opponent. And emotionally, it was the most exciting thing possible to be able to lock himself in a skin-to-skin embrace with a sweaty, squirming desperate athlete. All these elements collided and coalesced for him into a sexual thrill of such supreme pleasure he found nothing else in his young life to compare it to.

As they began the final round, Dean breathed deeply and employed his imagination to focus his thoughts again. Raul whirled around after a feinting kick, and for a moment Dean could see his back. In his tight electric-blue shorts, his ass jiggled while his plump ball sack was evident between his spread legs. Dean thought of one thing. He imagined slamming his opponent down and then forcing his cock deep into his mouth as he pinned his head with his thighs.

It was the motivation he needed. Thirty seconds later, the limber Argentinian offered Dean the chance he'd been waiting for. He struck out with his lightning-swift left foot, which put him slightly off balance. Dean snatched his ankle, yanking him forward and off his feet. He was instantly on top of him.

Dean had Raul down on his back with his big thighs between those deadly long legs and striking feet. He rolled him forward and thrust his crotch against Raul's powerful ass as they punched at each other in a flurry of strikes. Even amidst the intensity of the battle, Dean was totally aware of his cock pulsing beneath his shorts against the warm ass-crack of his sprawled opponent. This bout, like every fight, was unequivocally a sexual experience for the young red-head, even if there was no actual cock-sucking or ass-fucking.

It wasn't like sex for him, it was sex for him.

Raul was still striking effectively from the bottom, and Dean was not going to have a chance in hell of beating him unless he made his big move. He did. Rolling the Argentinian over, he clamped his arms around his opponent's and pulled back on his left shoulder. It was now or never.

Beneath him, Raul let out an explosive grunt of pain. Dean pressed down harder and pulled on the shoulder again. He knew this was his opponent's weak spot. He was well aware that three times before in Raul's fighting past that shoulder had been dislocated during a bout.

Raul had little choice. If he allowed another shoulder dislocation, it could be the end of his career. He chose to lose and fight another day. Groaning in agony, he tapped out.

Amidst the disbelieving tumult of the screaming crowd, Dean was declared the winner by tap out. He was the new welterweight champion

The Fuck

Dean came out of the shower with a towel draped around his waist to unexpectedly face the former champion there in his private locker room.

"What the hell are you doing here? Have you come to demand a re-match?"

That was what he would have done. He quickly noted that his manager and trainer had discretely vacated the room, undoubtedly to allow the two fighters some privacy for their post-fight conversation.

It was not completely out of the ordinary for the vanquished to visit the victor. It had only happened to Dean once and had been uncomfortable. He relished his wins and had trouble refraining from gloating when facing the loser. No wonder his friends in the combat sports community were few.

Raul smiled slowly. "Come. Sit here, and we will talk."

He spoke good English with only a slight accent. Dean wasn't impressed though, as he himself was a college graduate and considered himself as smart and educated as the next guy. He swaggered forward and planted himself on top of his trainer's massage table, which had been set up in the middle of the room beside where Raul had chosen to stand. The Argentinian had come in wearing only his sweats and his chest was bare. He'd obviously just finished showering and with the sweat and blood washed away, his golden skin and auburn hair were clean and glistening.

"So? Got something to say?"

131

The tall Argentinian stepped in close so that he was almost touching Dean's spread thighs. "Yes, my young friend. You should understand what happened out there. I tapped out because I believed it was better to submit now and fight again later. I am capable of long-term thinking whereas for you, it's all about right now"

They were eye-to-eye. As would be expected from two such strong competitors, neither shied away from the confrontation,

Then, Dean got the surprise of his life. Raul's hands came out to rest on his bare thighs just below the towel around his waist. He leaned in even closer so that they could literally feel each other's breath.

"I understand you like no one else can. You are so dedicated to your training you don't have room for anything else in your life. You believe winning is everything."

"Isn't it? That sounds like what a loser would say. What else is there?" Dean shot back, unable to back down even with those hot hands on his thighs and his cock rising to tent his towel.

Raul offered his slow smile again. Then, he leaned in even closer as he slowly slid his hands up Dean's muscular thighs, pushing up his towel until it bunched at his waist and his stiffening cock was exposed. Staring deep into the young red-head's eyes, he kissed him. A hand settled on his cock and pumped as his tongue slid between Dean's parting lips.

As startled as he was, it wasn't in Dean's nature to merely go with the flow. He struck back. He sucked in Raul's fat tongue as he reached down to tear open his towel. He then moved to seize his opponent's lean waist and pull him even closer while grinding his hard-on into the Argentinian's fist and flat belly. All at once it was like a clinch on the mat in the octagon, writhing flesh-to-flesh, and Dean was comfortably in his element.

His opponent met his aggressiveness with a quiet force that was irresistible. He allowed his tongue to be sucked deep, twirling it around inside the red-head's hot mouth. Raul opened wider, forcing Dean's mouth to do the same. Their lips gaped apart as their tongues dueled. They exchanged heated snorts for air, drooling over each other's chins as their lips smacked.

Raul's mouth pulled away with a loud slurp and slid downward, across his furry chin, down his smooth neck, across his pale chest to nibble at one nipple, then the other. Dean groaned and pressed into the mouth on his tit and hand around his cock. The mouth slid off the tender nub and traveled inexorably downward, toward the goal they both craved.

Dean's hands slid upwards along Raul's muscular back as the fighter bent over to bury his head in the red-head's lap. He held his broad shoulders and grunted as tongue danced over his jerking boner.

Raul licked up and down Dean's fat cock, slurping loudly while plastering spit all over the towering piece. But he wasn't merely content to offer up a lip-smacking suck-job. He looked up from his wet work, his dark eyes meeting Dean's brilliant green ones as he slid his hands under the red-head's knees and pushed back on his legs. When the fighter's ass-crack opened up, Raul dropped down to clamp his mouth over the exposed pink pucker he found there.

When those soft lips began to massage his tender hole and tongue slipped out to tickle the entrance, Dean's heavy body jerked wildly, and he found himself crying out. "Fuck! Oh fuck, oh fuck, oh fuck! Eat that ass, mother-fucker!!!"

Raul ate his ass with steady, mind-blowing deliberateness. He sucked, tickled and probed, then ran his tongue upward to the dangling sack and then the towering pole. He swallowed Dean's pink rod to the root, spit it out, then descended to attack his pouting hole again.

Dean's cock flamed pink, as did his puckered asshole. The two areas were bright beacons against the surrounding ivory-pale flesh. Raul attacked them. Back and forth, from hole to cock, Raul worked diligently without rushing as the red-head floundered on the table, feet in the air, grunting and shaking from head to toe. He tickled the hole with his tongue, teasing it open then slithered upward to trail along the length of the rigid shaft until he found the broad helmet and the piss slit. He tickled it just as he'd tickled the entrance to the hole then swallowed the entire hot pole to the balls.

Speechless for the first few minutes, Dean finally regained his bravado and spit out a challenge between gasps.

"You're so good with your mouth, ohhh, let's see what you can do with your ass! Take a ride on my cock, loser! Unless, ohhhhh, you can't take a big fucking piece like mine!"

Raul rose from his feast to face the flushed fighter on his back. He smiled, hardly fooled by the challenge. The young red-head's body had revealed his true feelings, writhing against his mouth rather than away from it, the hole blooming outward for his tongue, the cock thrusting upward into his mouth, the thighs trembling in his hands as they opened wide to allow him all the access he wanted. It was exactly like in the fight they'd just finished. Every time they had found themselves in the clinch, Dean had revealed his lust with the way he relentlessly clung to the lean Argentinian, and the way he thrust against him, undeniably relishing their body contact.

He didn't have to say any of that. They both understood. He smiled as he dropped his sweats to reveal he was naked beneath, his lengthy cock curving outward in all its honey-brown glory. He climbed up onto the table, pushing Dean backwards and reaching for the bottle of massage oil left conveniently at hand in a holder on the side.

His smile broadened as he squirted a stream of the clear liquid down over Dean's rearing pole. He squirted more on his fingers and reached back to rub the slippery stuff all over his ass crack. Dripping oil, he settled down over the sprawled fighter's lap.

They stared each other down as Dean clasped his hands behind his neck and waited. Raul gripped the base of the younger fighter's cock and held it steady as he sat directly on the plump knob. Slowly, he began to swallow it up with his clamping asshole.

Neither said a word as Raul steadily fed himself the full length of that quivering rod. When he had taken it to the balls, he slowly rose back up until only the flared head remained inside. Then he sat back down over it, smirking with pleasure as the prone red-head bit his lip and groaned.

It was too much for Dean. The sensation of that seething channel gulping in his aching rod, and the smirk on Raul's face as he teased him with his hot hole, undid him. He reached out and grasped the fighter's waist, holding him in place as he began to thrust upward in a rapid series of brutal gut-punches.

He'd half expected the kneeling Argentinian to grimace in pain or rise up away from the savage pummeling. But the opposite occurred. He grunted and squirmed, and his smile only grew broader as he actually settled down deeper over the drilling cock to take the slippery thing far up his gut without a hitch. His own cock rose up stiff and dripping from his crotch, signaling his pleasure in the brutal probing.

Raul's willing submission only made Dean want more. "Get on your belly and spread your legs, so I can really fuck your loser ass!"

His demand was met with gasping laughter but no argument. Raul rolled sideways, cock still buried in his slippery ass, pulling Dean with him. They wrestled momentarily as cock slid from hole and Dean forced the former champion to roll over again and settle face-down beneath him.

Unlike Raul, Dean did not believe in the slow and steady approach. He jabbed his knees between Raul's and shoved them wide apart. He snatched up the bottle of massage oil and squirted a stream of liquid all over the rearing mounds of Raul's warm brown butt. Scooping some of it up with his fingers, he barked out another demand as he stared down at the fighter's sexy can.

"Show me your hole, you fucking loser!"

Raul reached back and grasped the cheeks of his butt with his hands and spread them open. A hairless brown slot appeared down between the muscular globes. It twitched and dribbled oil but still looked tight and exciting.

Dean jammed a pair of oily fingers deep inside and twisted. Raul emitted a loud grunt, yet willingly reared backwards to take them. Then, to the red-head's amazement, he actually wriggled around the twisting digits to take them even deeper inside his churning ass channel.

The feel of that steamy chamber around his fingers only increased his greed to fuck it. He yanked them free and lunged forward to replace them with his cock. The thick tool, glistening with massage oil and bright pink, stabbed downward between the rearing honey-gold butt-cheeks. He planted both hands on Raul's shoulder blades and pinned him in place as he drove his cock into the fighter's puckered hole.

It gulped him in. Seething hot, slippery and quivering, the sphincter massaged his jabbing pole as he returned to the savage pace of his earlier pummeling. He slammed down into the snug channel, his white hips slapping against Raul's brown ass-cheeks. In and out, faster and faster.

The hole not only gulped him in, it quickly began to open up. Soon it was a gaping orifice able to take his driving cock to the root without any trouble. The total surrender of that steamy slot was exactly what Dean craved — and always had craved.

He fucked and fucked, while Raul egged him on in unintelligible Spanish. Dean understood *si*, but that was about it. It hardly mattered. Their communication was all about cock in hole, and there it was total.

Finally there came a point when Raul's lean thighs suddenly spread wider and his powerful ass reared higher, while at the same time his battered hole seemed to collapse inward in a total capitulation that allowed Dean's drilling cock to slam to the balls effortlessly. The pinned fighter swallowed the cock up his ass with a fierce greed that signaled the end. Dean knew what was happening even before Raul shouted it out.

"I'm coming! Fuck! I'm coming with your cock up my ass! *Si! Si! Si!*"

The words were music to his ears. Pinned to the massage table, Raul, the former welterweight champion, was shooting his load with Dean on top of him. He had fucked a load out of his opponent!

He rammed home again and again, feeling Raul's sphincter clamp and quiver with the power of his orgasm. He couldn't recall a moment in his life as sweet. He pulled out and stared down at the dripping, gaping hole he had fucked wide. He crammed three fingers deep inside it. As he twisted them around in the gooey cavern, he released a spray of nut juice all over the vanquished Argentinian's powerful ass-cheeks. Great gobs of creamy cum splatted the golden mounds.

Collapsing on top of the vanquished fighter, he started laughing, and so did Raul. Somehow they managed to roll around until they were face-to-face, leaking cocks smearing each other's bellies. A sloppy kiss finally smothered their laughter.

It was only later when Dean realized the momentous change that had occurred in his life that night. He had accomplished the biggest win of his mixed martial arts career, but what happened afterwards was where he learned the most important lesson of his life. Raul had shown him what it was like to be a good loser, and that submission was much more complicated and interesting than he had realized or understood before.

He would never be the same.

MOUNT OLYMPUS
By Jay Starre

Mount Olympus reared to the north, the snow-capped crown pristine against the cerulean blue sky. As they marched toward their fate that summer afternoon, the soldiers who tramped up the steep trail to meet their enemies imagined the Gods themselves watching from their perch on the sacred mountaintop.

Their journey was motivated by a dispute between the rival city-states of Thebes and Corinth. The warriors representing their homelands were compelled to travel north beyond Thessaly to the fabled slopes of Mount Olympus itself in order to settle this quarrel.

A score of men had been selected from each of the cities, and all were heroic specimens of their ilk. Each was renowned for his bravery in battle and also famous for his skill in the games, and one game in particular. Wrestling.

When they met, only three out of the twenty from each city would be chosen for this important contest. Every man longed for the chance to compete. For the glory of his city, naturally, but for his own glorification as well.

The meadow was sublime. Wild flowers in abundance dotted the plain, especially the wild tulips found here more than anywhere else on earth. Olive and cypress trees climbed the slope to the north while evergreen oak and redolent juniper crowded the southern perimeter.

A pair of lynx slunk off when the men appeared while a group of wild boar continued to root and snort just outside the forested fringe while maintaining a wary eye on the newcomers. The contingent from Thebes arrived first and took the high ground near the cypress grove.

There was only a brief delay before the Corinthians arrived. The adversaries eyed one another speculatively while their leaders conferred in the grassy space between them to begin the process of choosing the final contestants.

All the men were dressed in short tunics that fell half way to their knees and were girdled by thick leather belts from which hung their daggers and various leather pouches. The men from Corinth sported pale green while their opponents from Thebes wore golden brown. They wore leather headbands, even those with short hair, each tooled with their name and the names of their fathers.

Their sandals were uniformly discarded in preparation for the event, and they stood bare foot as the two leaders faced the lined-up men. Hermes, as Captain of the Thebans, spoke first. His deep voice rang out in the subdued peace of the alpine meadow.

"As agreed upon by our city's leaders, we will engage in three bouts to determine the winner of this contest. If no side is triumphant in all three bouts, there will be a second series of challenges to determine the overall champion. The contestants themselves are to be chosen in a pre-determined manner. As Captains, Zeno and I will choose first. Men, you must all strip down to your bare flesh so our choices may be made more readily."

The men obeyed without the slightest reticence. Each was proud of his body, and with good reason. In mere moments, forty entirely nude men faced one another across the field. The Captains strolled back and forth in front of the opposing teams and carefully eyed the competition. It was their opportunity to improve the chances of their city for victory and they must make a shrewd decision.

"I choose Antipater," Hermes proclaimed almost immediately.

The young warrior stepped forward and bowed to the opposing team. With glossy raven hair and dark brooding eyes, he looked menacing enough, but he was smaller in stature and less broad in girth than any of the other Corinthians by a substantial margin. The Captain from Thebes believed most of his men could overwhelm this one in a physical match.

Zeno took longer as he agonized over his own choice. The Thebans, other than a few outstanding specimens, whom he would never pick, were so much alike in physical dimensions there was no obvious solution to his dilemma. Then he noted one of the men sported a huge erection, and although hardly the only man among them to grow stiff in anticipation of the coming contest, there was something different about his hard-on. The curved weapon leaked pre-cum copiously, and twitched with an eager, almost uncontrollable excitement.

"I choose Nike."

As the young man stepped forward to bow to the Corinthians, a groan of dismay rumbled through his compatriots. It wasn't that he couldn't wrestle. He was a formidable athlete, but he had one major fault, which could be his downfall and a loss for his City.

One of the rules of the competition stated that it was not allowed to achieve an orgasm during the wrestling bout. If a wrestler ejaculates, he automatically forfeits. The Corinthian Captain had picked the one among them with the shortest fuse. Nike could hardly hold in the spew in his churning balls when pressed flesh-to-flesh with another hot and sweaty athlete!

The Thebans were given no time to bemoan their predicament. They must choose a wrestler from among the Corinthians for the second bout. There was little discussion and a swift and unanimous choice. "It will be Kleopatros."

The man was slender to the point of almost being willowy, although he was well-muscled nonetheless and rather tall. He did not appear to be the weakest, which might have been the logical choice if they wished to be victorious in the day's contest. So why had they chosen him?

Without a doubt, he was the most beautiful. In fact, his name meant "beautiful" and with his flowing golden hair, wide-spaced emerald eyes and bowed pink lips, he was divinely endowed with looks that took one's breath away.

The men of Thebes were looking ahead to the end of the contest and the aftermath. To the victors went the spoils, and every one of them wished to despoil this golden, glorious, beautiful Corinthian, Kleopatros.

Their Captain was the one to groan this time. The men had been blinded by lust! They should have picked a weaker man! But his hands were tied, and he could do nothing to alter the situation.

The Corinthians were well-pleased. They had much confidence in Kleopatros and bit back laughter at the foolish Thebans. Yet just as their Captain had, they faced a challenge to pick among the muscular warriors of Thebes for the least worthy.

There were two or three big brutes they could eliminate, and they finally zeroed in on the one who seemed the most timid. "We choose Panther!"

The Thebans finally found some solace in that. Panther was a shy and quiet young warrior, but he was unrelenting and stoic in battle and would not go down easily, even to the biggest and best the Corinthians might offer.

Now it was time for the men to choose among themselves for a hero. Appropriately, the Corinthians chose Heron, whose name meant hero. He was the tallest, towering over the rest, with long arms and legs and renowned for a fierce grip that was tenacious and cruel.

The Thebans had their own formidable weapon. "We choose Demon."

The man was not as tall as the giant Heron, but he was a brute. With broad and bulging shoulders and thighs like oak trunks, he often proved too heavy for his opponents to struggle out from under. Somewhat ugly with his huge nose and heavy brows, he had a sublime body of a human ox and the surprising smile of a glowing god. A coating of slick auburn fur accentuated his bestial appearance. His prick reared up like a knobbed club between his hairy thighs when he stepped forward, and the opposing warriors groaned. What a mighty tool!

The preparation for the first bout began at once. The three champions from each city were oiled up by their brethren. The honey-brown olive oil they used was slick and redolent, specially chosen from the pressing of olives off select trees in their homeland. It was a sacred substance.

They reverently rubbed and massaged their champions' muscular bodies, proud and hopeful that victory would be theirs. Every inch of the naked Greeks' bodies was coated, including their deep ass cracks.

The men grinned and winked at one another as they sported stiff members while engaging in this sensual prelude, and there was some lingering of hands and fingers as the champions were prepared. It was all in the spirit of the contest and none took offense, even when it was his prick and ass crack being slowly massaged by well-oiled fingers from a smirking brethren.

Once this was accomplished, the Captains had the men swear an oath to maintain their silence about whatever occurred that afternoon. Only the outcome would be revealed to their fellow citizens. Everything else would remain secret.

The location had been chosen carefully, particularly for the soft and spongy ground. A thick carpet of grass and flowers would help prevent bruising for the combatants. The first pair squared off as the others formed a large circle around them. Neither wrestler could breach that circle or he would be declared vanquished.

Antipater from Corinth and Nike from Thebes faced one another. Legs spread wide and leaning forward, they took hold of each other's shoulders and awaited the command to begin wrestling.

The ensuing fight, as all the following bouts, was extremely rough — and extremely sexual. Totally naked, with cock, balls and ass exposed and unprotected, there was no way to hide an erection nor prevent roaming hands from grasping sensitive, private areas. With nearly two score naked men watching, there were plenty of other stiff pricks under the afternoon sunshine.

The observing Greek warriors did not merely admire the male form, they revered it. And lust for their compatriots was not frowned upon. Actual anal and oral sex were taboo and even punishable by death, but taboo always has its allure. Among men who faced death in battle throughout their lives, the threat of such a punishment was not always enough to prevent them from engaging in many forms of forbidden lust. But in this public situation, even though the men swore an oath to secrecy, the rules were strictly enforced. Honor, as important as their lives, required them all to obey regardless of their secret lusts.

In any case, there were other ways to satisfy their sexual cravings between themselves. They did their utmost to do just that throughout the contest — and then especially afterward in the upcoming victory celebration!

In this first match, the raven-haired Antipater was the smaller of the two. The fair-haired Nike not only outweighed him, but had the longer reach. He was also more muscular with broad shoulders and powerful legs. Both had been liberally oiled though, and this turned out to be an advantage for the smaller Corinthian.

No eye gouging, deliberate scratching or any punching was permitted. Slapping though was allowed and encouraged as a way to gain points, especially if it was on the opponent's ass. Very quickly both Nike and Antipater sported fiery red nether cheeks. There was no biting, licking, or sucking allowed but groping, squeezing and tugging were not banned. It was Nike who took advantage of his opponent's splayed thighs as he pinned his chest with his large ass and then seized the pink pole rearing up between his legs. The wrestler beneath him grunted and squirmed as fingers pumped and squeezed his prick with maddening ferocity.

But Antipater managed to turn the tables on his opponent. First he reached up and jammed a hand between Nike's ivory-pale buttocks squatting on his chest. Next he wrapped his fingers around the Theban's plump ball sack and squeezed. With his big hand firmly surrounding Nike's slippery sack, he twisted and squirmed his way out from under the heavier man. Smelling victory, he maintained his grasp on those sensitive nads while he flipped the gasping wrestler around and around onto his stomach, his side, and finally his back with his long legs flopping in the air. It was like playing with a toy as the Theban grunted and wriggled around that relentless grip on his seed sack. He obviously enjoyed the pressure, because his hard-on swelled up into a rigid pink curve and suddenly erupted in a geyser of cum. He was vanquished!

The men surrounding the battle groaned and gasped, but were not permitted to encourage their champions or applaud the winner out of respect to both contestants. The disappointed Thebans gnashed their teeth and moaned but could do little else.

The joyous Corinthians smirked and winked, while one of their number even lost his own personal battle with lust and stifled a grunt of satisfaction as he let loose a spray of nut juice to moisten the grass at his feet.

The entire group found themselves stifling laughter at that but quickly turned their attentions to the next bout. The lovely Kleopatros from Corinth stepped into the circle to face Panther from Thebes.

Both men were blond and handsome. While Kleopatros smiled with glorious charm, Panther merely nodded silently. Both men were also smooth and glistened with a golden sheen under the afternoon sunlight. They looked to be an even match, and it was anyone's guess as to who would prove victorious.

Of course, the Thebans were aching to see the beautiful Kleopatros vanquished. Every man wished to savor the delights of his smooth firm flesh in the promised victory celebration!

It was a classic wrestling match. With legs locked over and over, muscular thighs strained. Shoulders bulged as both took turns pinning the other to the grass face down. With knees wide apart or feet in the air, delectable asses were spread wide, displaying butt cracks and holes that the watching men gawked at breathlessly. Of course hole poking was not allowed but rubbing and thrusting of genitals was perfectly acceptable, and both combatants took advantage of any opportunity to do just that. At times one or the other was upended, and their oiled hole palpitated wildly with their effort to free themselves. The Thebans moaned when their hero managed to thrust his erect prick between Kleopatros' rounded ass cheeks when he had him in that upended position. He rubbed the mighty weapon up and down the oiled crack and against the dangling balls and base of his stiff prick as the beautiful blond squirmed beneath him.

Quickly though, the Corinthian turned the tables and had his own prick shoved in Panther's smooth crack. Thrusting up and down the ivory pale valley, he did his best to distract his opponent and perhaps even precipitate a sudden release of pent-up cum.

Heavy breathing, grunting and groaning filled the air - the sounds of men engaged in a sexual combat that required every bit of effort they could muster to achieve a victory over a worthy opponent. And throughout the long battle, both men retained their erections. Especially Kleopatros, whose pink weapon reared and leaked continually as he fought. Many of the Thebans assumed he was on the brink of orgasm more than once, but they were proved wrong and soon despaired of that outcome.

The battle was so even, Kleopatros sensed his best chance lay not in outlasting the tenacious Theban, but in overwhelming him sensually. Rolling in the meadow grass, oiled limbs tossing and twisting, Kleopatros finally achieved the position he desired. Perched on top of Panther who lay on his back, the blond clasped both his opponent's wrists in a steel-like clasp, and stared down into his eyes with a gorgeous grin on his face. He began to writhe atop the pinned athlete. His lithe and smooth body massaged Panther's in a sensual glide, which would have been hard for any man to resist.

His final blow came quickly. Rearing his gorgeous round ass, he managed to find and capture Panther's stiff prick between his rounded ass cheeks. The oiled crack slid back and forth over the jerking prick with rapid and heated pressure. Pumping faster and faster, Kleopatros alternated between attacking Panther's prick with his ass crack and his own stiff tool. Mashing oiled pricks together in a slamming drive finally proved too much for the Theban. Flopping and grunting beneath the Corinthian, Panther cried out as he shot his load between their pressed bellies.

The second bout belonged to Corinth!

If the Thebans lost this final round, they would lose all. But they did not despair. They had Demon.

The brute stepped into the circle to confront Heron. The pair were opposites.

Demon was a stocky beast of glorious proportions. With auburn hair framing his brutish face and coating his enormous frame, he was a dark god who seemed to shake the ground with each lumbering step.

Heron was nearly a foot taller and longer in limb as well. Flaming red hair fell in waves to encircle a face with placid features and soft blue eyes. His body was also hairy, but the soft down of reddish fur was nearly invisible and only accented the smooth muscularity of his build.

When they locked arms over shoulders, it was hard to tell who would prove the champion.

Heron was no fool and battled ferociously to prevent his opponent from toppling him to the grass and burying him in his bulk. But Demon proved almost impossible to manhandle. He was just too big!

Their muscles strained in the sunlight. Heron's flesh glowed with a reddish glint while Demon's girth was a deep brown mat of oiled fur. It was the slippery oil that undid Heron. His grip failed him and Demon drove in to wrap his massive arms around the Corinthian's chest and thrust him backwards and onto the field.

The wind knocked out of him by the force of all that weight slamming down over him, he was unable to prevent the bestial Theban from twisting around and plopping his gigantic ass over his face. Demon reached down and seized the Corinthian's long thighs. He pulled them up and back to trap them in a bear hug to his massive chest.

The red-head flopped helplessly beneath all that bulk. He snorted in air around the furry crack that surrounded his face. His own ass-crack was wide open with the powerful cheeks spread. His asshole, surrounded by the faintest down of red fur, pouted outward as it danced helplessly to match his body's thrashing.

Demon chortled with delight, his club of a prick rearing up from his crotch in brutal glory. There was no way out for Heron. In a matter of moments, his struggles ceased as he found himself unable to catch his breath with Demon crushing him from above. He tapped the beast's furry thigh and it was over.

Demon proved himself a gentle winner as he immediately rose from his perch over Heron's face and turned to help the man to his feet.

The Thebans were awash with relief and a rising hope. Demon would have the chance to snatch victory from defeat for them now. To do so, he must fight the other two victors, and vanquish them both. Beating only one would not be enough.

He faced Antipater and the Corinthians despaired. Twice his size and hardly winded from his previous bout, the beast from Thebes faced the smaller Corinthian with a bright smile of pure glee. Antipater was brave, but once their arms had locked over shoulders, it was swift and decisive.

Demon lifted the smaller man off his feet with his gigantic arms. He raised him high in the air as the naked athlete flopped and thrashed before he slammed him down upon the meadow grass and immediately fell atop him. Buried under all that furry weight, the Corinthians struggles to free himself were fruitless. Demon finished him off by seizing both neck and knee in one mighty lock, which opened up Antipater's ass to the onlookers. His oiled hole oozed as he strained helplessly to free himself.

After a few minutes of that, with no escape forthcoming, Antipater was declared vanquished.

Now it was up to Kleopatros to wrench victory from defeat for his City.

The two faced off with arms on shoulders, both men smiling. Kleopatros gave no indication he was daunted by the breadth and girth of his mighty opponent. Demon's big paws clasped the slender Corinthian's shoulders in a firm grip as he practically oozed confidence.

Kleopatros did his best to prevent the giant from using his bulk against him. Over and over he slipped from the beast's grip, his smooth and oiled body aiding him in this. He slithered away from the clinch again and again as the lumbering Demon pursued him across the wrestling field.

Of course Kleopatros could not go far as they were surrounded by the others. Yet he did manage to score many points as he danced around the slower giant and reached out and slap his mighty buttocks again and again. The furry cheeks turned bright red.

For his part, Demon did not lose his composure, at least not yet. Relentlessly, he pursued and trapped the Corinthian, although Kleopatros continued to prove a slippery eel and escaped the beast's clutches.

Finally, the giant's massive arms surrounded Kleopatros in an inescapable grip. The blond responded by suddenly propelling himself upward and forward. Slightly off balance already, Demon toppled backwards. Unfortunately for the blond, the giant did not relinquish his hold even when they landed on the grass with a mighty thud.

Kleopatros used another trick to free himself. Squirming downward while reaching out with one arm, he insinuated a hand between Demon's furry thighs. Quickly, he sought out the beast's monster balls and took hold of them. He tugged and squeezed.

Demon let out a shuddering gasp, and his face grew bright red. But he did not give in. It took a harsh yank and a formidable squeeze to undo him. He jerked violently from head to toe then rolled away from the gripping fist and his slippery opponent.

Kleopatros was swift to take advantage and as the furry giant rolled onto his stomach, he leapt atop him and once more crammed a hand between his rearing furry buttocks. This time he found the monster prick and surrounded it with oiled fingers. He pumped the giant tool and squeezed it as fiercely as he had the brute's balls. At the same time he slapped the big furry ass cheeks with his free hand, racking up points.

Demon fought back. Rolling again, he twisted away from those hands and pulled the slender Corinthian beneath him. He sat down over Kleopatros face and pinned him to the grass.

When Demon's mammoth buttocks settled down over Kleopatros' face, the onlookers assumed it was all over for the handsome Corinthian. But he had more than one trick up his sleeve. Thrusting upwards with his feet, he managed to wrap them around Demon's neck in a feat of amazing agility. He then yanked downward with all his might. Even with all Demon's massive weight, the sudden explosiveness of the blond's feat managed to upend him.

He saved himself by rolling forward and away from his opponent. For a moment, the watching Greeks were allowed a glimpse of his pouting hole, hair-rimmed and snapping. The look on Demon's face was hilarious. His big dark eyes bulged, and his broad nostrils flared. He was obviously getting fed up with Kleopatros' wily tricks. Still, the blond was not done yet. He was quick to take advantage of the giant's confusion and leapt atop him from behind. He wrapped his muscular arms around Demon's neck and his powerful thighs around his waist.

It was quite a sight. The smooth pale body perched atop the hairy darker one, Kleopatros not much more than half the size of the Theban beast, and both with all their muscles straining.

But Kleopatros trickery was finally to no avail. Demon slowly rose to his feet, regardless of the arms and thighs encasing him. Eyes bulging and snorting for air, he wasted no more time and offered his clinging opponent the final blow. Pulling himself to his full height and then with a supreme effort actually propelling himself in the air backwards, he slammed his full weight down upon the blond.

The breath knocked out of him, buried under a mass of hairy flesh, Kleopatros passed out. It was over.

As the sun set two enormous bonfires were built on either side of the wrestling ground, which was now considered sacred. The defeated Thebans once more oiled up their champions, this time for the sexual bout that would follow. They wound flowers in their hair with their headbands holding the garlands in place.

The three vanquished Corinthians strode into the center of the encircling Greeks. Naked and dripping sacred oil, they wore only their headbands and the garlands of flowers.

The celebration about to commence would be a sexual bout, the victors having their way with the vanquished. With no actual penetration allowed, rubbing their bodies and genitals together would have to suffice. Yet with glorious bodies like these champions, that frottage would prove exciting enough!

It was Demon as Champion who would be allowed to frot first, and of course he chose Kleopatros to enjoy. The blond bowed with a surprising calm, especially considering the giant he faced and the club of a prick the man sported. He got down on his hands and knees as required and awaited his fate.

Fortunately well-oiled by his compatriots, his pink hole and deep crack flamed with an enticing flush in the flickering fire light. Demon's prick was a veined battering ram with a blunt apple-sized knob at the crown. He grinned with delight as he settled his big body behind the kneeling Corinthian and pushed his hairy thighs between the blond's slender smooth ones. His prick was also well-oiled and glistened in the firelight.

Every man watching held their breath as the dark knob settled between the blond's perky ass-cheeks and then pressed along the lovely crack. How would Kleopatros react?

The Corinthians knew their hero well, but the Thebans were in for a surprise. Before Demon had a chance to press his advantage, the blond heaved his lovely ass backwards. Emitting an explosive grunt, he began to fuck the mighty Theban tool with his slippery ass crack and buttocks.

"Yes! You are divine mighty Demon! Fuck me!"

The Thebans were totally agog as they witnessed the brutal battle that followed. Demon's grin only grew brighter and his eyes rolled back in his head as he battled against the blond's greedy body to take control of the ensuing contest. He lost, but with unmitigated pleasure.

It was amazing to see how Kleopatros' slender body thrust against the monstrous purple prick with wanton expertise. He fucked himself over the purple club with gyrating hips, slamming his pale buttocks against the giant's hairy thighs.

Demon seized those oiled hips and attempted to take some mastery over the blond's heaving body. But it was a feeble attempt. The pleasure of that slippery crack and the heaving buttocks against his throbbing prick could not be countered. He tried another tactic, sliding his massive tool up between Kleopatros thighs and thrusting it against his pink prick. He fucked that prick with his monster meat, faster and faster. But Kleopatros rode it with his own oiled tool, mashing downward over it. The slippery friction was almost volcanic.

Demon was undone. He shouted out his capitulation as his seed was ripped from his churning balls.

After this, it was a free-for-all. Every Theban intended on sampling Kleopatros' sumptuous body. Of course the tall and mighty Heron and the raven-haired Antipater were fucked by rubbing pricks against well-oiled crotches and limbs as well, and many times each. But it was Kleopatros who was offered the gauntlet of men who took him in every position and from every angle.

The gloriously beautiful Corinthian matched his opponents in every way. His lovely lips gaped wide as prick after prick slid between them. He nursed out load after load with grinning confidence. On his back, with a dozen oiled pricks rubbing over his thighs, belly and prick, he stole more squirting loads from his moaning, writhing opponents. He accepted them all, and milked seed from every contender. He himself achieved three orgasms, yet his curved pink prick remained stiff throughout the hours of his ordeal.

He seemed indefatigable. And above all, he remained gloriously beautiful even in defeat with cocks spewing on him and cum coating his shimmering body.

So it was at the end of the victory orgy, the satiated Thebans made a generous offer to the defeated Corinthians. As Captain, it was Hermes who voiced it.

"As victors, we are entitled to both Corinthian gold and ownership of the disputed lands in question. But in deference to the glorious bravery displayed by your champion Kleopatros, we offer to take a lesser prize. We will relinquish our claim over the land and take half the gold which is owed us. In exchange, we will take home with us Kleopatros himself. He will not become a slave, but will be welcomed as a hero. But he also must promise to become a loyal Theban."

The Corinthians groaned as one, but it was Kleopatros who stepped forward to speak. Still naked and sublime, he was calm as he addressed the gathering.

"As every Greek, I value my citizenship above all else. But our people are in much need of the disputed lands and poor enough that the lesser penalty of gold you offer will also be welcomed. I am only one man, and my city will survive without me. I accept on behalf of Corinth."

It was done, among some gnashing of teeth and open weeping in the ranks of the Corinthians. Kleopatros did not look back as he left with the Thebans, and every man among them knew it was to prevent himself from weeping at the last sight of his companions.

As dawn broke, the meadow was once more quiet. Sacred ground forever more.

BACKYARD RUMBLE
By Wayne Curry

Wayne Curry resides in the Midwest. Retired, he lives with his wife of nearly fifty years. He is a father and grandfather. Contact Wayne at waynecurry@outlook.com.

"What the fuck are you doing in my back yard?"

Looking up from my laptop, I was disturbed by the presence of a stranger who was talking on his cell phone.

I approached the dude getting between him and his only exit, the way he'd entered.

"Got to go," he said, as he flipped his phone closed.

He appeared as surprised to see me as I was to see him.

"I'm with the electric company; we're checking the lines in this area since the storm a few days ago," he explained looking me over.

I was wearing no shirt so my large tense muscles communicated my disbelief and served an intimidating warning.

He surveyed the enclosed yard as I circled to block his exit along the side of my residence; an area about eight feet wide between the house and the fenced-in property line. A six-foot privacy fence cordoned off the entire backyard area. The gate through which he'd gained entrance remained unlatched and open.

I shook my head negatively. "I don't believe you," I said. He wore athletic shoes and a baseball cap turned backwards, not standard attire for a service repairman working utility lines. "Stay right there," I ordered, fumbling to find my cell phone.

He looked as if he wanted to run. "Don't move you're not going anywhere," I warned more emphatically the second time.

"Look, old man," he addressed me. "Back out of the way. I don't want to hurt you. But I will if I have to."

He was younger than I by a few years and appeared to be an excellent physical specimen, but I wasn't afraid. "Look, punk, I'm not playing games," I stressed. As a bodybuilder and wrestler, I was accustomed to aggressive guys and considered myself to be one of them.

I had just stoked up on my breakfast carbs and was feeling my oats so to speak before moving to the patio for my morning coffee and glance at the online headlines; my typical activity for an early Saturday morning. A mild summer day, I wore no shirt or shoes but had managed to pull on a pair of snug fitting shorts to partially cover my lower anatomy. Dressed casually and not really expecting this event, I hadn't planned my wardrobe.

"Let's get something straight, pal," I said. "This's my house, my property, my backyard, and you don't belong here," I stood firm, my feet planted wide, "You're trespassing." I thought I'd presented my case reasonably well. "Until you can come up with a good reason to be back here, you're not going anyplace."

As expected, I did not have my cell phone with me; par for the course when I needed it.

"Look, don't make this more difficult than it needs to be," he said. "I've done enough time, and I'm not going back for more. Now, you obviously know how to swing the weights around," he stated referring to my stature, "but so do I." He ripped off his T-shirt.

The fact that the dude chose to remove his shirt in this circumstance indicated that he wanted to make a statement. As a bodybuilder about my size, he was well put together, and he intended to prove it. It quickly became evident that we were going to fight.

Without hesitation, he charged in my direction to get past me to the gate.

I was surprised at how quickly the adrenaline kicked in. My reaction was to block his escape. Minus any forethought, I changed levels, dove forward, and wrapped my arms around his thighs. I hadn't lost it. I lifted him up and slammed him to the ground completing the tackle. As we tussled, I came out on top. Again I was surprised. After an absence of years, it felt good to make hard physical contact with another dude. Today, I felt supercharged.

He landed rights and lefts from the bottom like a man who was accustomed to fighting off his back. The force of his blows told me that his hard jail developed muscles served him well. I postured up and struck back in retaliation with the intentions of busting him open. Fortunately, I trapped his right hand that was inflicting most of the damage allowing me to pound away to his left side. It began to come back to me. Two to the body followed by one to the head. I got into a rhythm and gained strength just from remembering what to do.

I looked into the eyes of my adversary. The dude was smiling at me. He was enjoying himself as much as I was. That's when I decided that there was no holding back; no saving up for later; I really wanted to turn it on just to take it to the next level; to wipe that shit-eating grin off his face.

Maybe he had the punching advantage, I calculated, but I had the edge in the wrestling.

My success on top was short lived. Wedging an arm under my leg, the dude tilted me off-balance and tossed me to the side long enough for him to escape out from under me and roll to the top. Driving my head into the ground, he found it convenient to pound several fists to my jaw. Dazed by his heavy hands, I was unable to think clearly.

Recognizing his advantage, the dude jumped to his feet and attempted to flee. By some quirk of fate, I grabbed for his leg before he could get a way. Able to snag the bottom of his torn Levis with one hand, I tripped him causing him to fall to one knee beside me. He struggled to pull free.

Rolling to my side, I looped my arms around both of his legs and held on. My action brought him totally to the ground apparently causing him to change his escape plans. He mule kicked free from my grasp and turned in my direction. As he struggled to his feet again, rather than running away, he now appeared hell bent on staying behind to finish me.

Diving down on top, he kneed me in the abdomen several times landing hard knees to my breadbasket. One was low just missing my nuts. He made up for his miscalculation. His hard hand grabbed in the vicinity of my cock and balls and squeezed. This time, he scored. While I was immediately persuaded that he could run away without any resistance, the dude evidently was enjoying his change in heart. He apparently relished watching me squirm in pain and wanted to inflict more of it.

While I know most men respect the male genitals as off limits in a fight, there's no known etiquette in a serious scrap. Since he broke the ice, I felt some lee-way for my spontaneous retaliatory plan. Because he'd set the precedent by going for my nut-sack first, I felt that the accommodating thing to do was to go for his.

As my hand made contact with his privates, I could tell that he was supercharged by the fight. His rod filled his pouch. I grabbed a fistful of meat and squeezed holding on. His tolerance threshold was remarkable. He'd apparently learned endurance in prison.

"You son-of-a-bitch," he exclaimed before peppering my face with a barrage of un-targeted punches from on top. "Don't fuck with me," he warned. Although my left eye was now receiving the brunt of his attack, my nuts still ached, and I wasn't prepared to argue.

"You're not taking me seriously, dude," he admonished. "I will hurt you," he stated matter-of-factually.

Other than lifting weights and bodybuilding, there was nothing better than a good fight, and I was in one. To prohibit any further damage to my balls, I struck upward with my bare foot from my back. I landed a kick catching him on the chin, and he went stumbling backward head over heels. I rolled to my feet and was again positioned between him and his escape route.

He came at me with a front kick that I caught and held on to. I trapped his left leg against my ribcage as he hopped to retain his balance on one foot. I held securely to his ankle and worked my way forward pulling him in my direction. When I had him close in, I smiled, imitating his shit-eating grin and raised my left knee in a threatening gesture. Attempting to avoid the inevitable, he tugged harder to free up his foot. There was fear in his eyes. Still retaining the smile on my face and with his nuts in my cross-hairs, I fired my knee squarely striking its target. His supporting leg folded under him, and he fell with his full weight to the ground.

Diving in to take advantage of my top position his legs wrapped around my head. Before I could fire off one blow, he tied up my hands. I knew he was in pain from the shock to his nuts, and he acted erratic. Having withstood everything that I'd thrown in his direction, the fear in his eyes was diminishing and being replaced with determination. I also knew that I had to do something dramatic to break his will.

Although in pain, we both were enjoying the nastiness of the fight. I recognized that I was no longer concerned with the intruder's reason for being in my backyard nor was I anticipating anyone's help in subduing him. I was now fighting for the pleasure and the excitement involved, and the goal of imposing my will while beating up a nasty bastard. We were appreciating that two hard asses were having fun destroying each other. My muscles were responding. They found satisfaction in beating the fuck out of the dude.

With his legs above my shoulders encompassing my head and neck, he was able to trap my arm in a triangle choke. Keeping the trapped arm bent at the elbow with the assistance of my other arm, I managed to get to my feet, lifting the dude off the ground as I stood. As he hung near the ground, I swung around slamming his head into a nearby concrete retaining wall. The force of the blow caused him to release his legs from around my neck and he fell to the ground in a heap. Instantly I was on him inflicting as much damage as I could with my fists. One of us was bleeding. It was me.

I have to admit, straddling another muscular dude balled up on the ground pounding on his muscles was a pleasurable experience. It was not just his head that I wanted to punish. As I rolled him over, I looked down on his chest breathing heavily beneath me and was overcome with the desire to pound his rugged body. Targeting his left pec first, I released a barrage of punches to the fleshy mass. When he tried to grab my hand, I moved to his head and pounded his eye. When that disturbed him, I switched hands and targeted his right pec. Getting the better of the brawl was good, but understanding that my adversary had been toughened up by prison life made the event something special. I was punishing a mean dude.

The tussle continued for several more minutes when I thought I heard a police siren in the background. Again the dude had gotten to his feet and came charging at me with a flying knee as I changed levels looking for a single leg takedown, but this time the stranger anticipated what was coming and momentarily defended his position.

Landing a strong knee to his body, I drug the fight back to the ground landing in the guard of the stranger, but persistently, he worked his way to his feet, nearly giving up his back in the process. I immediately tried to take him back down.

The dude dug a powerful hook into my body, and I tried to clinch. The stranger lifted me up and slammed me down sideways onto my head staggering me. The dude locked his legs around my head in a figure four head scissors.

The two of us lay exhausted on the ground in a tangled mess of limbs.

"Alright you two, break it up," a loud voice ordered.

I looked up and saw a policeman standing above us. "Which one of you lives here?" he asked.

"I do," I offered, breathing heavily.

The policeman separated us.

"What's going on here?" The policeman asked.

Attempting to catch my breath, I offered an explanation. "He's trespassing," I panted. "I caught him wandering around in my backyard, and he wanted to fight. He says he's done jail time."

"Well this is your lucky day," the policeman revealed. "This dude is an escaped felon with a record as long as your arm." He slapped cuffs on the stranger's wrists. "He's doing time on a homicide rap. I guarantee he's up to no good."

"He's a big boy," I offered, beginning to catch my breath.

"He escaped by beating up a couple of armed jail guards two days ago. You must be a bad ass to contain him until we got here," the policeman commended.

His comment made me feel good. "Really," I expressed my amazement. "Who called you?" I asked.

"We got a 9-1-1 call from an elderly neighbor lady," the policeman revealed. "She reported two men fighting in the backyard at this address," he added. "Apparently this dude was actually looking for her," he continued, "but he got the wrong house. They'd just talked by phone before she saw the fight."

At a loss for words I starred at the policeman bewildered. "That's who he was talking to when I saw him."

The policeman continued, "She's his grandmother that he hasn't seen in twenty years."

RASSLIN' YOUR ROCKS OFF
By Wayne Curry

Normally when out of town on a job, Gill Martin and I share a hotel room for the project's duration. While our company provides us a per diem travel allowance, by doubling up on the room, we're able to pocket a few extra dollars.

The arrangement works well. Gill and I have a lot in common; we share similar sport's interests and are both amateur bodybuilders. We have season tickets to hockey and football games and work out together at the same local gym where we encourage and spot each other as partners. Married, we each have two children and are traditional husbands in the family structure; not without our faults but able to remain married after enduring several years of trials and errors. Besides being close friends, we also share another thing in common, we are brothers-in-law through marriage. Bros, if you will in more than one way.

All of that aside, Gill and I are highly competitive. For example, on a recent out-of-town job, I awoke early in the morning … it was not yet daybreak … as Gill rose quietly from his bed and made his way in the darkened night to the bathroom. I glanced at the clock on the stand between our two beds. It was only 4:30 a.m. and quiet outside.

Before doing his business, Gill closed the bathroom door, but I could still hear him as he whizzed to conclusion. It was on his return to the main part of the room, that he left the bathroom light on and the door ajar so a ray of light emanated through the otherwise darkened quarters. The soft glow allowed him to carefully make his way through the maze, stepping among shoes and soiled clothes haphazardly strewn on the floor. After all, as roommates, we were guys who didn't pay particular attention to housekeeping details.

In the dim light, I observed my muscular bro-in-law catching sight of himself in the dressing mirror. Pausing to check out his reflected image — a typical bodybuilder activity — he couldn't resist striking a few poses and admiring his flexed physique. Besides wearing a set of identification tags around his neck and a thick gold banded watch on his left wrist for practical reasons, his bikini style underwear resembled classic bodybuilder briefs, which added to the posing platform fantasy apparently playing out in his mind. He adjusted his male gear by rearranging his package and pulling the bikini lower, so it subtly revealed his pubic hair line in preparation for the pending exhibition. Not totally satisfied with the mirrored image, he tugged at the briefs, lowering them to reveal the base of his cock and permitting ample room for his protruding basket to expand.

What ensued was not just a quick perusal of his physical attributes and flawless physique but a rehearsed posing routine with one pose followed by yet another in a display of graceful male pulchritude. Gill inhaled, filling his lungs with air and began to perform his routine with what's called the bodybuilder's relaxed pose, a misnamed stance requiring the exhibitionist to assume a full frontal position with arms cocked outward to the sides in a somewhat poised but stiff presentation. With his legs spread, more or less shoulder width apart, he slowly and deliberately tightened and clinched both fists as if grabbing ahold of something in each hand. He methodically raised his bent arms up toward his head flexing his forearms and both biceps as he struck a front double biceps pose, which he held for a few moments.

The loose fitting chain-linked bracelet on his right wrist slipped downward before abruptly being blocked by his knotty forearm.

Then, placing his left hand behind his head and glancing to the right, he opened his mouth wide expressing an amazed look as he starred at the overwhelming size and shape of the huge, tightly flexed bicep directly before his eyes. After pausing for a second or two of admiration and worship, he continued raising his right arm still higher in the air bringing the huge mounded bicep mass to his puckered lips to kiss the enlarged bicep belly.

With a grinning facial expression, he reversed his attention, turned his head to the left, in the opposite direction, and emphasized a similar movement with his huge left arm. As part of his staged presentation, he flexed the left bicep, licked the mounded surface, savoring its texture with his roving tongue, barred his clinched teeth, and made a biting, gnawing gesture in an animalistic, self-ravaging of the massive muscle.

Studying his image face forward in the mirror, Gill lowered his arms and made a large circling motion bringing his hands together under his chest. Turning to the right in a side chest pose, he inflated his lungs with air and flexed his pecs, tightening and twisting the muscle slabs to accentuate the strands and striations. Sighing as if totally infatuated with his appearance, he held the pose and starred, looking approvingly into the mirror at his muscular perfection.

Repeating the earlier circling motion with his arms, he bought both open hands to rest behind his head, and stepped face forward with one foot. Tightening his abs and flexing the protruding leg's quadriceps, he hit a front abdominal pose, which he twisted and turned causing the side oblique muscles to pop into prominence. After prolonging the pose, Gill smiled broadly, as if expressing reassured satisfaction. Freeing one hand from behind his head, he wiped it across his abdominal bricks further tightening them with each sweep of his hand. Veins running in haphazard directions seemed to crawl across the surface of his cut-up, contorted stomach.

Again, he made a large sweeping movement with his clenched fists and arms bringing them to rest at his waist. Raising his chest in the air and flaring his back muscles to their maximum, he slowly struck a front lat spread, which he held for his own scrutiny. Still gazing intently in the mirror, Gill arched his arms and fists, and stepped forward into a front most-muscular stance to end his routine. Breathing hard, after completing his self-admiration, he observed his total vascularity and pumped physique and nodded his head in satisfaction and approval.

I broke the silence with my applause.

Caught off-guard by the surprise, Gill turned around to see me lying in my bed on the far side of the room, wide awake. Recognizing that I was conscious, he asked boldly, "How long have you been awake and watching?"

"Since you got out of bed to take a piss," I replied, stroking my hardening cock and chuckling to myself.

Although embarrassed by being caught in his self-worship fantasy, Gill didn't let it bother him. "I can tell you like what you see," he stated, "there's no hiding that." Directing his attention to the blossoming boner between my legs, "Look at that," he explained, pointing in my direction. "That thing's blood red," he added, referring to the purple tip of my cock head. "Apparently, I've captured your attention. What is it, bro?" he asked. "You wanting to fuck these muscles?"

"Nope," I quickly replied. "I don't fuck guys," I chuckled, adding a laugh to my comments. "Besides not being the right gender, you wouldn't know how to handle a real muscle stud on you." My rock hard cock was throbbing in the air as I spoke.

"Well, either you like what you see or you need to go drain that thing. You've got some serious morning wood," Gill concluded. "And taking a piss," he paused before finishing his sentence, "presents you with a BIG challenge," he stated with emphasis. "You'll have your hands full."

"What challenge," I asked?

"You've got to get past these muscles," Gill said, referring to himself, "to get to the bathroom. And you'll piss all over yourself before you make it."

I laughed again. "Feeling rambunctious, aren't you?" I asked. "Sounds like you're the one who wants to fuck someone this morning," I concluded. "I think you're over estimating your abilities. Aren't you, stud? You don't seriously want to wrestle these muscles. I'll have those muscles," I pointed in his direction, "and your ass," I emphasized, "pinned to the floor in sixty-seconds or less. If I was an ass fucker, you wouldn't know what hit you. Even though you've got some impressive muscle there, bro, I'm certain about one thing. You really don't want to test your wrestling skills with me," I said confidently.

"It's not a test of my skills," Gill replied self-assuredly, before pausing. "When these muscles tie you up, it'll be a test of your will. You'll be hurtin' fuckin' bad, bro. First, I'll lock you up, then, I'll fuck you up," he added gleefully, emphasizing the latter part of his comment. "Fuck you up without fucking you," he added, self-confidently.

"Oh really?" I questioned. "Get your trinkets off, mutha-fucker, and we'll see how wicked you are," I ordered, pointing at Gill's jewelry.

He anxiously complied by removing his watch, disconnecting his bracelet clasp, and lifting the identity tags from around his neck. He then moved his hands to the bikini briefs, voluntarily dropping them to the floor, stepping free and kicking them aside. He stood there stroking his meat as it was beginning to harden also. "Anything goes, fucker?" Gill asked.

"Agreed!" I replied, accepting the game play.

"Get rid of that shirt," Gill ordered. "I want you raw."

"Fuck you," I replied. Since a T-shirt is all I normally wear to bed, "You want it off?" I asked; "Come take it off." I opened my arms wide beckoning with my hands for him to approach my bed where I was leaning back on several pillows resting against the headboard. With my legs spread wide; my hard-as-a-rock cock, pointing straight up at twelve-o'clock, and a smile on my face, "Bring it on," I commanded. "Come to daddy; take your beatin'."

It took Gill less than a split second to react to the invitation. He lurched forward, threw himself on me and the grab-ass started. Hell bent on getting my T-shirt off as I'd challenged him to do, Gill pulled at it until it ripped into shreds, leaving us both totally nude to wrestle on the bed sheets. I was equally hell bent on spearing him with my hardened man-sword and pulled him into me with that intention.

We rolled over and over twisting each other in contorted positions until we both fell off the bed onto the floor. Pillows were strewn everywhere. We laughed and quickly got to our knees still searching for an advantage. Suddenly, Gill dove at me again. Driving his shoulder into my waist and lifting my butt up off the floor, he forcefully threw me onto his bed which quickly became the mat for our muscle fight.

The tussle was not only a test of strength between us but a venue for the body worship that muscle hounds and bodybuilders are in to. Gill's hands roamed my body, enjoyably stroking my chest and arms and fondling my manhood. I in turn, took the opportunity to explore and feel the hardness of his masculine body armor including his back and glutes. Testosterone was flowing in each of us as the male aggressiveness surged.

Wrestling holds were a combination of high-school and college grappling, professional wrestling and mixed martial arts. In the heat of the anything goes exchange, it became clear that whatever worked, worked.

While exchanging blows, both of us engaged in some serious grappling tactics in an attempt to submit our opponent. We each wanted to pin the other man's ass or make him beg for release. When I had Gill rolled up in a small-package hold, his hand found its way toward my manhood. Feeling and exploring beneath my hardened cock, Gill grabbed my balls in his tight fist and menacingly tugged on my nut-sack stretching it far beyond its natural size and proportion. In fear of being permanently injured, I released my hold and grabbed for my privates attempting to secure and preserve them for posterity. Once I was free, it was his turn to wrap me up and constrain me in a similar predicament.

In one move, I laid between Gill's legs on top of him in the Jujitsu "open-guard" position. My arms were wrapped around his head and neck as I scrambled to apply an arm-in triangle choke hold. As he raised his legs to the small of my back and crossed his ankles closing his guard, he pulled my midsection into his crotch where I could feel the moist head of his blood engorged cock rubbing against the hard bricks of my stomach.

"Yeah, fuck my abs, stud," I whispered in his ear. "You like my hard gut, don't you? Keep at it. Fuck my abs hard. Fuck'em raw. They're tight, aren't they? Just the way you like'm. Go after them. Get your rocks off, bro. Get your hard rocks off on my abs."

Recognizing the possible predicament in which I had my opponent, I attempted to improve on my advantage. Lowering the weight of my body into his crotch, I forced air into my stomach and rolled my abs smashing Gill's cock against my gut muscles. "You're getting close, bro, you're ready to fire," I whispered. Momentarily he stopped fighting as the agitating activity massaged his blood sated cock against my rock hard abs. An audible gulping sound from his lips communicated that my actions were having a profound effect on his willpower. "Give it up," I told him. "You know these muscles are too much for you. You can't hold it much longer. You love the feel of my muscles crushing your manhood into submission, don't you? There's plenty for you, have some more."

While Gill didn't want to yield to my wrestling prowess, the pleasure of my actions on the tip of his throbbing cock head were causing him to groan from the ecstasy he was encountering. So pleasurable were his sensations that he began to undulate on his own, in effect masturbating his cock using my hard muscular abs as a stimulus. "Give me your rocks, bro," I ordered, "give me your rocks," threatening again and again.

Meanwhile, as I controlled my rival's cock from the top, underneath I took the opportunity to strategically position my knee at the base of his testacies. As he became aware of the increasing juices building up in his penis reservoir wanting to be released, Gill grabbed a hand-full of my hair with his free hand. "Now, you'll pay, fucker," he moaned, tugging at my head.

"Suck it up," I told him. When the time was right, I deliberately nudged his balls with a menacing tap of my knee. Painfully audible sounds escaped from his throat as he gulped for air.

"Fuck," he verbalized.

"Pain or pleasure?" I asked. "Which is it? Make up your mind. It's your choice."

When Gill did not respond, I encouraged his decision by kneeing him in the bare nuts again; this time harder.

Gill released my hair allowing me to return to the cock rubbing abdominal gyrations that were driving him into a sexual frenzy. "Wise choice," I quipped. "All your smarts are in your balls."

What had started as a playful school-boy tussle was gaining in intensity as we became more engrossed and enraged at our inability to submit the other man. Meanwhile, the body heat between us was growing more intense and the sweat became more profuse.

Desperate to escape, a sudden explosive burst of strength from my powerful roommate, propelled me off his bed. Before I knew what happened, I was back on my own bed with my head buried between his bicep and forearm in a tight headlock with him lying across my chest on top of me. With his free hand, he grabbed a pillow and plastered it over my nose and mouth. "Now, it's your time to suffer; cock sucker," Gill uttered. "Now, I'm in charge, you muscle mutha-fucker. And, that means I'm taking your rocks, bro. Your cock belongs to me. Got that? I'm taking your juices, bro, everything you got is mine."

Still struggling for air, I grabbed the pillow with a free hand and threw it on the floor.

Gill, in turn, clasped his two hands together and twisted my neck in a contorted configuration not intending to extend any chance of freedom to me. With his full weight on top of me, he cranked my head upward toward his huge chest where his right pectoral was only inches from my face. Sweat dripped from his tit into my eyes. Applying still more pressure he lowered his massive pec smashing it into my nose and mouth, in effect, replacing the discarded pillow with his sweaty pec slab. With a rubbing motion, he ground his chest into my face blocking the air flow and effectively prohibiting me from catching a breath.

"Oh you'll love this," he said. "Suck on my tit, dude," he chuckled. "Take it all. It's yours; all yours." He rolled the huge muscle mound over my nose and mouth. "You can have everything you get from it, bro. Suck on it. Suck it dry."

Resisting, I pulled back gasping to capture a breath.

"I said suck it, bro," he ordered as he continued to forcefully engulf my nose and mouth with the massive muscle slab. "Nice!" he exclaimed. "Oh yeah, bro, I love this. Take it, bro, taste the brine. Lick it, bro," he said. "You like my sweat, don't you? I know that I like the feel of your damp, hot breath on my tit," he added, rubbing the nipple into the saliva and perspiration around my lips.

"Suck on the whole thing; all of it. It's big enough. Take as much as you want, there's plenty of it for you, bro, and look. Here's another one to spare," he said, referring to his other muscle tit.

Obligingly, I took the nipple of his pec into my mouth where I first tonged it several times before squeezing it between my firm lips.

"Yes," he confirmed.

When I had it hardened and moist, I sucked on it and tried to draw it between by teeth. Positioning the nipple along the upper and lower rows of teeth, I bit into the kernel like tit with the intention of inflicting as much pain as I could. The anguish on his face expressed the sensation that he felt. "Fuck!" he yelled. He quickly released his clasped hands and slammed his fist into my jaw. He followed up by shoving his pec back over my mouth, as if positioning his tit for more abuse.

But before he could inflict any further damage, I slipped out of the neck-crank. My escape was aided by the perspiration flowing from the two of us making it difficult for either of us to hold on to or control the other man. Using my free hand, I reached to grab his wrist and any other body part that I could locate. At the same time, I rolled out from under him as he turned toward me attempting to maintain the advantage. I hurriedly threw a leg over his midsection as we lay facing each other on our sides. Without hesitation, I plowed a right fist into his open gut which was unencumbered by his arms or legs. From there I was able to mount my brother-in-law and land several solid punches to his face. My hardened fists found their mark.

When he tried to bridge up and buck free, I advanced my position by moving upward on his chest where I enveloped his head with my legs in a figure four head lock. Similar to the triangle choke, the hold is an MMA submission specialty.

Tightening the leg lock, he had little room to turn away. Gill's reddening face starred directly at my massive hard-on. His mouth, located in front of my ball sack, was panting. His heavy breathing caused his hot breath to be exhaled directly onto my ballooning testicles. I used the predicament in which he was placed to restrain him as I cock-whipped his face with my hard man tool.

Leaning back, I reached for his cock and began to stroke it furiously. My intention was to force him to ejaculate. With my legs wrapped around his head, my left hand whipping him with my cock, and my right hand effectively jacking him off, the game was almost over. "Oh, yeah, fucker, now you're mine." Finally, I was in control, or so I thought.

While reaching back jacking Gill, my body was off balance. Gill executed a leg lift raising both legs high into the air up toward my head. Able to wrap one leg around my neck, he pulled me backward, and flipped me off the bed onto the floor for a second time. A split second later, Gill rolled off the bed and sat facing me with our legs interlocked. We began striking each other.

Sharing each other's laps, we swung our fists with blows to each other's face, nose, and jaw. Blood began to flow from both. We exchanged punches to the chests and abs.

Suddenly Gill reached up and pulled my head down to his and held on tightly effectively bringing the fight momentarily to an end with our heads side-by-side.

We were both, breathing hard, sweating profusely and bleeding. I rubbed the stubble of my morning beard into his.

"Bro," he whispered in my ear, "I love fighting you." With his free hand, Gill grabbed for my cock and began jacking it.

"I know," I answered. "I know." I reached down between our legs and grabbed his throbbing dick in return. "And, I'm not done with you, fucker."

With each other's cock in hand, we began furiously jacking the other man.

In minutes, we were each reaching our climax and neither wanted to stop. We wanted it rougher. As I stroked my brother-in-law, I twisted his rock hard dick producing painful pleasures. "Oh, fuck," he cried out.

In retaliation, my brother-in-law squeezed my cock harder, and bent it as if breaking it off.

In the midst of sweat, blood and pre-jizz, the climax built. I could feel the release coming in my cock. I knocked his hand away from my cock and grasped both cocks with my single fist and squeezed our two dicks together. I looked him straight in the face and twisted both cocks. The mounting pressure began to burn as the juices rushed to the tip of our blood gorged dicks. Veins in both tools strained to their max as the tension mounted in preparation for the coming eruption.

While both of us desired the impending climax, neither of us wanted the build-up experience to end. Finally, the explosive moment arrived when cum began to erupt freely. Both of us released a flow of expletives. "Oh, fuck, fuck, fuck," we exclaimed almost in unison. Cum squirted in streams and cascaded abundantly from both piss slits as it drained down the sides of the two cocks, covering fingers and fists.

The two of us rested, nestled together in each other's blood and sweat and engulfed in each other's arms. My hand rubbed the juices from both cocks together covering our cocks, balls and lower abs with the warm, slimy fluids. My brother-in-law soaked his hand in cum and smeared it over my pecs. I responded by rubbing a glob of cum into his bloody face.

"That's quite a rock collection you got there, bro," Gill proclaimed, as the tension eased.

"God, that was great," I added. "That was a truckload of rocks; a landslide," I paused, before urgently continuing.

"Now, get off me, mother-fucker," I ordered. "I've REALLY got to take that piss."

THE VANQUISHED OPPONENT
By Mark Apoapsis

MMA is Mark Apoapsis's favorite spectator sport, for all the wrong reasons. Mark has no website at the moment but may be reached at mapoapsis@excite.com]

I'd heard what he'd said at the pre-fight interview: "I'm going to break his spirit," my buddy's opponent had boasted. But they all say things like that. Brian himself had made equally dark and equally empty threats in return against ... Mike somebody-or-other. I couldn't remember the guy's last name, just that the announcer had introduced him as Mike "the Merciless" Somebody, stretching the last name beyond the point of intelligibility.

Brian held his own during Round 1; he was fast enough on his feet to dodge blows, although he didn't land any solid ones himself. His much rangier opponent's reach advantage meant that every time Brian closed the distance between them, warily defending his square jaw with one gloved fist while winding up to throw a punch with the other, it left his torso vulnerable to blows a split second before he got within his own striking distance. And he always looked unnervingly vulnerable to me to begin with, stripped down to his shorts and facing off against an equally strong and skilled man who had permission to try to hurt him as much as he could until the referee decided to call a stop to the fight.

Brian had a spectacular-looking spinning kick, which he tried twice, but it didn't quite connect, any more than his left hooks and uppercuts. In return, he absorbed a few glancing leg kicks and body shots, but avoided the rest. The round ended with both fighters unbloodied. Both gleaming with sweat from head to foot, though, so that Brian's sparse chest hair, curly when dry, was slicked down in muscle-hugging patterns, the way it looks when he's just stepped out of the shower.

I had a ringside seat not far from Brian's corner. His corner had spent most of the round yelling at Brian, "Take him down!" But so far, Brian had chosen to kept the fight off the ground. In the break between rounds, while mopping Brian's brow and chest with a towel, his corner must have convinced him, because just seconds into Round 2, he ducked under an attempted roundhouse punch, wrapped his arms around Mike's torso, lifted him off his feet, and slammed him to the mat. I started cheering, as did the guys around me; this whole section was rooting for Brian. Mike instantly wrapped his long legs around my buddy's waist, which always looks slightly obscene to me but is the standard way of guarding against being put into an even more defenseless position. Brian managed to pin one wrist to the mat, exposing Mike's hairy armpit, and I tasted a brief moment of thrilling anticipation of watching my friend render his opponent helpless and force him to submit.

He decided to give him a pounding instead, or maybe he just wanted to soften him up before trying to hook an arm around his neck. He jabbed his elbow into Mike's shoulder a couple of times, then raised his gloved fist above his face. But Mike snaked his free hand around the back of Brian's neck and forced his head to his chest in an embrace that was probably a lot less friendly than it looked. He held him there, Brian's nose practically buried in his armpit, while he looked over at his corner for a signal.

Between his head being trapped, and the ankles crossed in the small of his back, there wasn't much Brian could do, despite being on top. His blind jabs had no leverage behind them. Then, with a sudden heave, Mike rolled them both over onto their sides, legs still locked around Brian's waist. He loosened his grip, allowing Brian to struggle up onto his hands and knees. Quickly, Mike jumped onto his back, hooking his arm around his neck so that Brian's throat was in the crook of his elbow. This time he somehow managed to get his long legs wrapped around Brian's meaty arms, pinning them to his sides, something very few fighters are limber enough to do. He spent the next several seconds working to flatten my buddy out on his belly. Then he forced Brian to again roll onto his side with him, as if proudly presenting his catch to the audience. I had a good view of Brian's familiar muscular chest, heaving as he fought for oxygen. Brian's mouth was open, revealing his red mouthpiece.

There was plenty of time on the clock as Mike started slowly exploring Brian's exposed torso with his fist. It was starting to look like I'd flown all the way to Las Vegas to see my best friend beaten to pulp. But I could tell that the blows were just hard enough to hurt, not designed to crack ribs or even cause much bruising. I think Mike the Merciless was just making a point: he had Brian completely helpless and unable to defend himself. The referee was watching carefully and seemed to be thinking about stepping in.

Finally Mike did what I would have expected a fighter do as soon as he's mounted an opponent's back: he stopped using his free hand to tenderize the muscles of his defenseless opponent's chest and arms, and hooked it in back of Brian's head, grabbing his own biceps, so that Brian's neck was trapped in the triangle formed by his arms. It's called a "rear naked choke." I'd once looked up the origin of the name. The fighters were of course only half naked, but apparently it's the only strangulation hold from Jujutsu that works when the fighters are bare-chested. In other words, they're naked from the waist up, and that's what counts.

I could see Mike squeezing his elbows together, and Brian's face turning red. I knew that the pressure on both sides of my friend's neck would be cutting off the blood supply to his brain and that within seconds he would submit, knowing he was beaten.

Except that he couldn't submit. Normally a fighter signals submission by repeatedly tapping the mat, or if that's not possible, patting his opponent's bare skin. That's because often, like now, he's in no position to verbally submit. But Brian's arms were completely immobilized by Mike the Merciless's legs. No way to tap. I watched as he went limp, eyes rolling up.

Mike held on anyway, grinning triumphantly. He was wearing one of those white and black mouthpieces made to look like the guy had shark's teeth and was prepared to tear into a nice beefy shoulder as soon as he immobilized his opponent. I'd seen those on several other fighters and always felt were pretentious and looked even stupider than plain mouthpieces do.

The referee peered at Brian's limp form then jumped in and pulled Mike off, waving to signal the fight was over.

# # # # #

"This is bullshit," Brian argued after Mike's hand was raised, as trainers and medics and cameramen and sportscasters crowded into the ring. I didn't have access to enter the ring, but I climbed onto the edge and leaned in, hoping to shake my friend's gloved hand, or more satisfyingly, clap him on his bare shoulder; I could get away with that much. But he was focused only on his opponent.

"This is bullshit," he repeated when Mike and his corner had finished an enthusiastic embrace. "I never tapped out."

"Only because you couldn't. You couldn't do shit. I had you completely immobilized. Anyway, you lost consciousness."

"No, I didn't! I remember everything."

"Dude, I felt you go limp in my arms. Anyway, if you weren't already out cold, you would have been, in a few more seconds. I had you, man. I was in deep. There was only one way it could end."

They were still rehashing the same arguments when they reached Brian's dressing room, with me tagging along feeling increasingly like someone's neglected puppy. I think Brian would have followed Mike right into his dressing room to continue the argument as Mike changed out of his trunks, if Mike hadn't obligingly stopped when we got to Brian's.

"If the damn ref didn't stop it, we'd be fighting Round 3 right now. I could totally have broken out."

"Look, man, you should be grateful the ref was there. He was the only thing that kept me from using you as a punching bag for as long as I wanted, and then choking you out within an inch of your life and holding your limp body up in front of your little buddy here and all your fans." He gestured at me.

"Bullshit!"

"OK, man. You think the fight would've ended differently without a ref? Keep your gloves on and come to my hotel room in half an hour, and we'll continue. No ref, no rules, just you and me." He poked Brian's bare chest to emphasize each phrase. "Room 1355."

# # # # #

"Dude, you're not really going to take him up on it, are you?" I protested when I saw he was about to leave the dressing room having only put on a T-shirt and shoes after pulling his sweat pants directly over his trunks. He still had his gloves on, the officially inspected and initialed tape undisturbed. Mixed-martial arts gloves aren't heavily padded and closed like boxing gloves; they leave a guy enough dexterity to get his clothing on and off if he wants to, although I've noticed that some fighters still opt to have an assistant take off their T-shirts for them as they enter the ring.

"Swear you won't tell anyone, man. I could get in a lot of trouble, even if I don't hurt him bad. But I plan to hurt him bad. Or at least humiliate him."

"Is it really worth risking an injury when you've got another fight next weekend?"

"I wouldn't be in this sport if I was scared of getting hurt."

"Normally you get paid for that!" But it was no use arguing with Brian when his pride was at stake.

# # # # #

Brian was letting me share his hotel room. We were staying all week, since he was fighting on back-to-back weekends. He had promised we could have a little fun in Vegas in between. We'd been friends since high school. He'd often protected me from bullies who'd seemed about twice our size. I don't know what he got out of our friendship back then, but since then I'd helped him through some hard economic times until he'd earned a contract, from letting him crash on my couch to paying for countless pizzas. Nowadays, he really seemed to like having me there rooting for him. Just not giving him sensible advice.

When he wasn't back an hour later, I started getting pissed that Mike was stealing the evening away from us, when I should have been getting Brian good and drunk. It might be our one chance before he started preparing for his next fight. When another hour went by, I started getting worried. He'd left his phone in the room, which meant I had no way to reach him. That also meant he wasn't in the casinos or shows, or out on the town. He would have come back for his phone, and a shower and change of clothes — and for me. That could only mean he was still alone with Mike. Or, as I kept phrasing it in my mind, in the hands of Mike the Merciless.

I didn't have Mike's mobile phone number, of course. I learned later that it's possible to call another room in the hotel from the land line in the room, but I'd barely noticed that our room had such a relic from the past, and I'd certainly never read the instructions. I'd never needed to call a hotel guest whose mobile number I didn't know. So I went up and knocked on the door of room 1355 in person.

# # # # #

The room Brian shared with me was luxurious enough, but Mike somehow rated, or could afford out of his own pocket, an entire suite of rooms.

"You didn't exactly answer my question," I said as Mike stood aside and gestured me in. "Is he here or not?"

"He did come up here, a couple of hours ago, to continue the fight like I offered," he said as he closed the door behind me. "Your friend is a real hothead, you know that? To hear him talk, you'd think the state Athletic Commission's safety rules are for sissies. That they take all the fun out of the sport for real men."

"Yeah, Brian's always been like that," I agreed. "When did you say you last saw him, again?" I gathered the fight had ended some time ago, since Mike was now dressed in casual street clothes, was bare-handed, and wasn't sweaty.

"I, on the other hand," he continued, ignoring me and opening a dresser drawer, "much as I wish I didn't have to wear one of these things, appreciate that it's better than getting my teeth knocked out." He held up a red mouthpiece. "Let alone these." He fished a jockstrap out of the drawer and dangled it in front of me. "I mean, is there anything manly about leaving your balls swinging loosely for your opponent to accidentally graze with his toe? But I sort of agree with your buddy Brian about one thing. Choking a man into unconsciousness is way more satisfying than watching him tap out. Beating him senseless is much more satisfying than a

194

TKO, where the ref steps in and says," and here he affected a dry academic tone I'd never heard an actual ref use, "'I can see at this point there's nothing he can do to stop you from striking him until he's unconscious, so let's pretend you did.'"

"What are you saying? That you sent him to the hospital?"

"I didn't send him anywhere."

A chill ran down my spine. "Please tell me he's alive," I whispered.

"Of course he's alive! I'd never kill a man I had at my mercy! And I'm in complete control; I know how long I can safely cut off his blood supply at any one time. It's a lot longer than a ref would let me. Always stopping the fight before I can savor my victory! I can't even hold a guy helpless on the mat for half a minute without the ref warning me he's going to stand us up if we don't 'work.'" He toyed absently with the jockstrap. "And then there's the most frequent and annoying warning of all: 'Let go of his shorts!' Well, there was no ref here tonight."

"Wait ... Brian was the one wearing a red mouthpiece. Yours was ... Wait a minute! Is ... Is that his jockstrap?"

"Finally!"

"He took off his jockstrap to fight you?"

"No. He didn't."

"Then ..."

"I took it off him. Not during the fight, of course. Only after I defeated him."

"He'd never let you take ..."

"What part of 'defeated' don't you understand?"

I gaped at him, dumbfounded. Finally I said, "Is he still here? Is he all right? Do I have to carry him back to our room?"

"He's in the bedroom, and he's fine. A little sore, but nothing broken. Except his spirit, of course."

Bastard. "I want to see him. Are you going to try to stop me?"

"I could, of course." He squeezed my shoulder, a friendly gesture under most circumstances, but I got the feeling he was assessing my musculature and assuring himself he could take me if he wanted to. Which is not why friends squeeze each other's shoulders. I don't think. "You're not a fighter, are you?"

"Not professionally ... Well... No, not at all," I admitted.

"You're not secretly a fellow black belt?"

"No. But please, can I just ..."

"Don't worry. I like the idea of his friend seeing him like this. Come on in."

With a casual grip on my all-too-unremarkable biceps, he guided me into the suite's bedroom.

196

# # # # #

I gasped at what I saw, though I should have expected it after the jockstrap. My buddy was stark naked, spread-eagle on his back on the bed, with his wrists bound over his head by ropes tied to the headboard. Ropes stretching from his ankles down to luggage on the ground ... luggage that seemed to be stuffed full of handheld weights ... kept his legs spread. He was conscious, but a gag in his mouth kept me from finding out what he had to say for himself. His well-muscled body looked pathetically vulnerable stretched out like that, with his hairy armpits ... which I knew to be extremely ticklish ... wide open, and his almost hairless ball sac lying loose, draped over a fold in the rumpled sheet, completely unprotected, looking every bit as fragile as it was.

"It looks like he really didn't want you to see him like this," Mike said gloatingly, interpreting Brian's expression the same way I did. He walked over to stroke my helpless buddy's bare chest possessively, playing idly with his chest hair. Brian barely tried to recoil, but his ball sac had contracted the minute his captor approached, drawing his balls protectively against his body. His nipples also shriveled up, like a conditioned response. I noticed an ice bucket lying on the nightstand.

"OK," I said shakily, "you've had your fun. Now let him go."

"You think you can make me?"

"I can report you to ... I don't know, the organizers? The state commission? You'll be thrown out so fast ..."

Brian looked much more alarmed at this threat than his smug captor did, shaking his head vigorously and protesting through the gag.

Mike said, "Everyone's in this sport for a different reason. My reason is that I love utterly humiliating my opponents in public, laying them out right in front of the TV cameras. I don't care about the money or fame. If you report this, it'll be all over the media and the web, I guarantee it. Everyone will know what I did to Brian here. He'll never live it down. That would be better than anything I could have hoped to accomplish in the rest of my career. So go ahead. It'll be so totally worth getting thrown out."

"I can come back with some of Brian's other friends, who are fighters." I named three of them, one of whom fought in the heavyweight division and could probably mop up the floor with Mike singlehandedly. But again, Mike just smirked while Brian's eyes got wide, and he shook his head emphatically and moaned what was unmistakably "No!" through his gag. His cheeks were red.

"Go ahead, call them right now. I'd gladly risk any beating they might give me, just to see the look on their faces when they see what I've done to their buddy. If I weren't willing to risk getting hurt for the chance of humiliating an opponent, I wouldn't be in this sport."

In rage and frustration, I did an incredibly stupid thing. I lunged forward and took a swing at Mike. He caught my wrist, twisted my arm around my back, and the next thing I knew my throat was trapped in the crook of his elbow, my cheek was squashed against my buddy's chest, and his curly chest hair was tickling my nose. Black spots started swimming before my eyes, slowly blotting out the close-up view I had of Brian's nipple about an inch from my face.

I felt Mike's hot breath in my ear. "Do you want to wind up tied naked to the bed beside your friend?"

"No," I managed to choke out as he eased up on the pressure.

He picked me up and shoved me away so that I went sprawling on the floor at his feet. "Then don't come back. He's mine now. Don't worry, I'll let him go eventually. When I'm done with him."

Brian tried to say something around his gag. "What was that?" Mike removed the gag.

"I submitted to you, you bastard! Over and over!" I'd never heard so much shame in his voice. "What more do you want?"

"You admitted you were beaten and completely helpless. You haven't submitted. Not to everything. And if your friend doesn't leave right now ..."

"Leave him alone!"

"... I'm going to force him to stay and watch me wring every remaining shred of pride out of you."

# # # # #

I lay awake all that night, keenly aware of the empty bed beside mine, wondering what I should do. Brian seemed to be more worried about everyone finding out he'd been briefly enslaved than he was about remaining a slave until

Mike tired of him. It was just like him! And yet, he had another fight coming up. I knew his career meant a lot to him, and his record. If he didn't show up for the weigh-in the day before, he'd forfeit the fight. If he didn't spend the week staying in condition, he'd be trounced. Lying in a bed all week, flat on his back ... or whatever positions Mike the Merciless was forcing him into ... would leave him in no shape to fight.

The next morning, after finally grabbing a few hours of fitful sleep after dawn and then a quick shower and no breakfast, I was back outside Mike's suite, banging on the door. Mike, already full clothed but still unshaven, opened it and yanked me inside by my shirtfront.

"You're back," he said, closing the door behind me. "And alone, which is smart if you want to keep Brian off the front page and the video sites, but not so smart if you care at all about yourself. Because now you're fair game. I warned you." Keeping a vise grip on my biceps, he frisked me with his free hand, none too gently. "Did you really think you could rescue your friend singlehandedly, unarmed? It's not even one against one, by the way. My friend Matt is here. Turns out he's scheduled to fight Brian this weekend, if I let him go."

"This isn't a rescue attempt. It's a ransom offer."

"I've got all the money I need. But a vanquished opponent as a slave, a plaything? Priceless. Well, as long as you're here, come on in and see how Brian's training is coming along. We've been training him to improve his submissions, you might say. And working on his conditioning, in the sense that ..."

"I get the picture."

When he opened the bedroom door, I saw Brian, head hung in shame, kneeling naked at the feet of a man I remembered seeing publicity photos of. Matt was in the middle of buckling his belt. I noticed reddened areas that might have been lash marks on Brian's bare shoulders, and one across his chest.

I hung back as Mike entered and filled a glass from a pitcher and held it to the kneeling prisoner's lips. Brian drank thirstily. He placed his hand on the glass to steady it, but Mike kept control of it as he drained it, his Adam's apple bobbing visibly. Brian hadn't shaved this morning, either. Or been shaved. That made four of us.

My friend wiped his lips, lowered his head again, and to my horror, said meekly, "Thank you, master."

Mike tousled Brian's hair, almost affectionately. "I take good care of my slaves, don't I?"

"Yes, master," he said, not raising his chin from his chest.

"Look who's back," Mike said, moving aside. Catching sight of me in the doorway, my friend looked mortified, blushing and covering his genitals with his hands. Not that it was anything I hadn't seen many times in the years we'd been buddies, in locker rooms and showers, in hotel rooms and camp tents ... but I guess there was shame in having been stripped against his will.

"Who's this, slave?" Matt demanded.

"My best friend, sir," Brian said miserably, head bowed.

"Dude!" Matt said to Mike. "We should make these two ..."

"I'm here to negotiate!" I interrupted, backing away.

Mike slid behind me and put his meaty hands on both my arms, preventing escape. Not only was I surrounded by two bigger men, both trained fighters, but also I couldn't even see one of them. And the man I'd always been able to count on to watch my back, literally and figuratively, was kneeling naked at the other bully's feet, watching helplessly.

"I don't see a flag of truce," Mike said, leaning so close I could feel his breath on the nape of my neck.

"What?"

"A white flag." He reached around me and clasped his hands together in an unbreakable grip, pinning my arms to my sides. "When you go behind enemy lines for a talk, if you expect your enemy not to take you prisoner, you have to carry the international signal of truce, even it's just a makeshift piece of cloth."

"Uh, if you could lend me a pillowcase or something ..."

"The pillowcases aren't white."

Matt walked up to me and said, "But I see you've got something that is." He hooked a finger under the neckline of the T-shirt beneath the open collar of my shirt. "Will this do,

Mike?" I tried to back away, but Mike was like a solid brick wall, an unusually warm one, against my back.

"I'd accept that," Mike said, resting his chin on my shoulder. "Help him out, would you?"

Slowly, unhurriedly, Matt began unbuttoning my shirt.

# # # # #

"Your armpit hair is almost as bushy as your buddy's," Mike said delightedly. "I don't suppose you're half as ticklish? No, don't worry. I won't touch you as long as you're carrying the flag of truce." He gripped the neckline of the T-shirt he held and strained until it ripped down the middle then thrust it into my hands.

I reached for the shirt Matt was holding. "Could I have ..."

"We took this off you before you had a white flag," Matt pointed out, tossing my shirt on the floor behind him.

"You wanted to negotiate," Mike said. "Start talking."

Twisting the remains of my T-shirt nervously in my hands, I said, "Well, you did say you were going to let him go by the weekend anyway, so he could fight Matt."

"I didn't say that. I said 'if' I let him go. Matt, what have you decided? Do you want to fight this guy?" He stepped over to Brian, who was still on his knees. He hadn't even attempted to come to my aid, just knelt there, watching with tears of shame running down his face as I was forcibly stripped to the waist. "He won't have trouble making weight, that's for sure. I haven't been feeding him." He squatted down and ran an appraising hand over my unresisting buddy's ribs.

"What's the point?" Matt said. "Look at him. He's got no fight left in him at all." He kneed Brian in the back and forced him to lie with his face in the plush carpet, then planted his sneaker casually on Brian's broad, muscular back. "Keep him as long as you like, bro. If the fire sprinklers didn't have that no-hanging warning on them, I'd suggest you string him up to use as a human punching bag."

"Maybe when I get him home. You'll help me load him into my trunk on Sunday, won't you?" He reached down to slap Brian's ass.

"Look," I said, "if you won't accept money, is there anything else ..."

"How about a trade?" Mike said immediately. "Would you be willing to take your friend's place?"

Brian howled incoherently into the carpet and tried to rise. "So he does have some spirit left," Matt said delightedly, forcing him back onto his belly and grinding his face into the carpet.

I swallowed hard, but said, "In a heartbeat. I'd do anything for Brian."

# # # # #

It felt like I'd been a prisoner for months, but it had only gotten dark around the edges of the curtains five times, and Mike had made less than a dozen trips to refill the bucket of ice that supplied one of the least intense and intimate of the torments he'd been inflicting on my naked body as I lay spread-eagle on the bed. He'd fed me twice and shaved me three times. Just my face; although he'd threatened each time to shave various parts of my body while he was at it, that was the one threat I didn't really believe, even when he went so far as to spread shaving cream all over them. I could tell he enjoyed playing with my body hair too much. He'd only shaved twice himself: once when his stubble had grown too long and soft to cause pain when he rubbed his chin over my reddened skin, and once tonight before going out.

Mike had been gone for an unusually long time this evening. When he came back, he was gleeful. "Your buddy just lost to my buddy in the first round. Submission due to rear naked choke. I feel like celebrating."

I groaned, knowing what his idea of a celebration was. My only consolation was that everything he did to me was an indignity I'd heroically spared Brian from, which made me feel good. Brian was going to owe me big-time. Maybe that's why, in a twisted sort of way, I was almost starting to enjoy this.

"And you know the best part?" Mike sat down on the edge of the bed, near my outstretched leg. "Matt got him to agree to the same thing that started all this. He's down the hall in Matt's room now, to finish the fight without a referee. Some people never learn."

I whimpered in abject despair. All this for nothing! Remembering Matt's rough hands all over me these past few days while Mike held me down, I could vividly imagine those hands getting reacquainted with the bound and naked body of my recaptured buddy at this very moment.

"I think I'll buy him from Matt after Matt gets tired of him," Mike gloated, toying with my pubic hair. "I could use two slaves. I loved the look on his face when he watched me take you down and strip you down to your undershorts and work you over, just before we let him go. Imagine forcing him to watch what I'm about to do to you now. Better yet, what if I force ..."

I heard the door to the suite open in the next room. "That must be Matt now," he said. "He's the only one I gave a key to."

But to my surprise, it was Brian's voice I heard calling out from the outer room, clear and strong and self-assured: "I brought a white flag."

Clad in trunks and a T-shirt, he strode confidently into the room ... at least, as much as a man can stride when he's carrying a bundle on his shoulders that weighs exactly as much as he does. "And some trade goods," he added, bending down to let his heavy burden tumble to the floor. He yanked away the white sheet, revealing a dejected-looking Matt, hogtied and gagged, utterly defeated, and utterly naked.

ng any underwear. "Excuse me," I said, having a hard time looking
ed by that bulge in his crotch, "but don't I know you?" "Maybe,"
of t   bout a m
Ray   God, you
er?   in?" he a
"Lik   s stronges
ody   e on Gree
he l   I ever sa
to t   any ideas
king   he same
coul   ery long
raci   ne swell.
with   e in store
go c   behind s
ee u   in public
' he   vent to th
cy.   grabbed
d. I
raci   t, so firm
t, ha
h my   bing dick
ng, I   n cock, b
ound of unzipping filled the small space. I don't know who's hand
t before I knew it, I had his rod in my hand, and mine was in his. "
do?" he asked, his tone challenging. I knew exactly, and sank to

BUTCH MEN PLAY HARDER!

BUTCH DIXON